# *Mountain idylls, and Other Poems*

## *Alfred Castner King*

# Contents

# MOUNTAIN IDYLLS, AND OTHER POEMS

BY

Alfred Castner King

*TO THE MANY FRIENDS WHO HAVE SO
KINDLY ASSISTED IN THE ARRANGE-
MENT
OF THE MANUSCRIPTS FOR
PUBLICATION, AFTER THE SHADOWS
OF HOPELESS BLINDNESS DESCENDED
UPON ME FOREVER, THIS VOLUME
IS AFFECTIONATELY DEDICATED*

# PREFACE

*"Of making many books there is no end."--Eccles. 12:12.*

When the above words were written by Solomon, King of Israel, about three thousand years ago, they were possibly inspired by the existence even at that early period of an extensive and probably overweighted literature.

The same literary conditions are as true to-day as when the above truism emanated from that most wonderful of all human intellects. Every age and generation, as well as every changing religious or political condition, has brought with it its own peculiar and essentially differing current literature, which, as a rule, continued a brief season, and then vanished, perishing with the age and conditions which called it into being; leaving, however, an occasional volume, masterpiece, or even quotation, to become classic, and in the form of standard literature survive for generations, and in many instances for ages.

Poetry has always occupied a unique position in literature; and though from a pecuniary stand-point usually unprofitable, it enjoys the decided advantage of longevity.

The mysterious ages of antiquity have bequeathed to all succeeding time several of earth's noblest epics, while the contemporaneous prose, if any existed, has long lain buried in the inscrutable archives of the remote past.

The two most notable of these, the Iliad and the Odyssey, are believed to have been transmitted from generation to generation, orally, by the minstrels and minnisingers, until the introduction or inception of the Greek alphabet, when they were reduced to parchment, and, surviving all the vicissitudes of time and sequent political and religious change, still occupy a prominent place in literature.

The Book of Job, generally accepted as the most ancient of writings, now extant, whether sacred or secular, was doubtless originally a primitive though sublime poetical effusion.

The prose works contemporaneous with Chaucer, Spencer, and even with that most wonderful of literary epochs, the Elizabethan age, are now practically obsolete, while the poetical efforts remain in some instances with increased prominence.

Someone, (although just who is difficult to determine,--though it savors of the Greek School of Philosophy,--)has delivered the following injunction: "Do right because it is right, not from fear of punishment or hope of reward." Waiving the question as to whether it is right or not to compose poetry, he who aspires in that direction can reasonably expect no material recompense, though the experience of Dante, Cervantes, Leigh Hunt, and others, proves conclusively that poets do not always escape punishment. In fact, about the only emolument to be expected is the gratification of an inherent and indefinable impulse, which impels one to the task with equal force, whether the ultimate result be affluence or a dungeon.

The author of this unpretentious volume has long questioned the advisability of adding a book to our already inflated and overloaded literature, unless it should contain something in the nature of a deviation from beaten literary paths.

Whether the reading public will regard this as such or not is a question for the future to determine, as every book is a creature of circumstance, and at the date of its publication an algebraic unknown quantity.

It was not the original intention of the author to publish any of his effusions in collective form until more mature years and riper judgment should better qualify him for the task of composition, and should enable him to still further pursue the important studies of etymology, rhetoric, Latin and Greek, and complete the education which youthful environment denied.

On the 17th of March, A.D. 1900, occurred an accident in the form of a premature mining explosion which banished the light of the Colorado sun from his eyes forever, adding the almost insurmountable barrier of total and hopeless blindness to those of limited means and insufficient education. At first further effort seemed useless, but as time meliorates in some degree even the most deplorable and distressing physical conditions, ambition slowly rallied, and while lying for several months a patient in various hospitals in an ineffectual attempt to regain even partial sight, the following ideas and efforts of past years were gradually recalled from the recesses of memory, and reduced to their present form, in which, with no small hesitation and misgiving, they are presented to the consideration of the reading public, which in the humble opinion of the author has frequently failed to receive and appreciate productions of vastly superior merit.

*Ouray, Colorado, March 15, 1901.*

# Grandeur.

Dedicated to the mountains of the San Juan district, Colorado, as seen from the summit of Mt. Wilson.

I stood at sunrise, on the topmost part
Of lofty mountain, massively sublime;
A pinnacle of trachyte, seamed and scarred
By countless generations' ceaseless war
And struggle with the restless elements;
A rugged point, which shot into the air,
As by ambition or desire impelled
To pierce the eternal precincts of the sky.

       Below, outspread,
A scene of such terrific grandeur lay
That reeled the brain at what the eyes beheld;
The hands would clench involuntarily
And clutch from intuition for support;
The eyes by instinct closed, nor dared to gaze
On such an awful and inspiring sight.

The sun arose with bright transcendent ray,
Up from behind a bleak and barren reef;
His face resplendent with beatitude,
Solar effulgence and combustive gleam;

Bathing the scene in such a wealth of light
That none could marvel that primeval man,
Rude and untaught, whene'er the sun appeared,
Fell down and worshiped.

A wilderness of weird, fantastic shapes,
Of precipice and stern declivity;
Of dizzy heights, and towering minarets;
Colossal columns and basaltic spires
Which pointing heavenward, appeared to wave
In benediction o'er the depths beneath.

Uneven crags and cliffs of various form;
Abysmal depths, and dire profundities;
Chasms so deep and awful that the eye
Of soaring eagle dare not gaze below,
Lest, dizzied, he should lose his aerial poise,
And headlong falling, reach the gulf beneath.

Majestic turrets, and the stately dome
Which, ovaled by the slow but tireless hand
Of eons of disintegrating time,
Still with impressive aspect rears its brow
Defiant of mutation and decay.

The crevice deep and inaccessible;
Fissure and rent, where the intrusive dike's
Creative and destructive agency
Leaves many an enduring monument
Of metamorphic and eruptive power;
Of molten deluge, and volcanic flood;
Fracture and break, the silent stories tell
Of dire convulsion in the ages past;

Of subterranean catastrophe,
And cataclysm of internal force.

The trachyte wall, beseamed and battle scarred;
The porphyritic tower and citadel;
The granite ramparts and embattlements
Of nature's fort, impregnable and wild,
Stand as a symbol of eternal strength,
And hurl a challenge to the elements!

Canons of startling and appalling depths,
With caverns, vast and gloomy, which would seem
Meet for the haunt of centaur or of gnome;
The gorgon and the labyrinthodon;
The clumsy mammoth and the dinosaur;
Or all gigantic and unwieldy shapes
Which earth has seen in the mysterious past,
Would seem in more accord and harmony
With such surroundings than the puny form
Of insignificant, conceited man.

And interspersed amid these solemn peaks
Lie many a pleasant vale and grassy slope,
Besprinkled with the drooping columbine,
And fragrant growths of all harmonious tints,
Whose variegated colors punctuate
Grandeur with beauty, and fearless, bloom
In the forbidding shadow of the cliffs,
And to the margin of the snowy combs
Which still resist the sun's persuasive ray.

A lakelet, cool, pellucid and serene,
Fed by the drippings from eternal snows,

Lies like a mirror 'neath a frowning cliff,
Or as a gem, majestically ensconced
In diadem of crag and pinnacle.

Down towards the distant valley's sultry clime,
Both solitary, and in straggling groups;
In solid phalanx, rigid and compact;
In labyrinth of branches interspread,
Impervious to the rain and midday sun;
In form spontaneous, without regard
To law of uniformity, there stand
In silent awe, or whispering to the breeze,
The sombre fir and melancholy pine.
And many a denuded avenue
Of varying and considerable width,
Cut through the growth of balsam, spruce and pine,
Which stands erect and proud on either hand,
Attests the swift and desolating force
Of fearful, devastating avalanche.

# SCENE IN OURAY COUNTY, COLORADO.]

The mountain rill its pleasant music makes,
As the descendant waters roll along,
In rhythmic flow and dulcet cantabile,
In various concord and harmonious pitch,
Pursuant of its journey to the sea;
The murmuring treble of the rivulet,
Uniting with the deep and ponderous bass
Of torrent wild and foaming cataract;
The thunderous, reverberating tones
And seething ebullition of the falls

Are blended in one grand euphonious chord.

Far in the hazy distance, as the eye
With vague perceptive vision penetrates,
Lie the vast mesas of ethereal hue,
Stretched in a calm and sleepy quietude,
Dreamy repose and blue tranquillity;
The eye which rests upon the drowsy scene
Beholds a dim horizon, which presents
No line of demarcation or of bounds;
A merging union, blurred and indistinct;
Fuliginous confusion, that the eye
In viewing gazes, but no more discerns
Which is the earth, and which the azure sky.

But mark the change!
A cloud, which floated in the atmosphere,
An inconsiderable and feathery speck
Of no proportions, now augmented, wears
A threatening aspect, ominously dark;
Enveloping the heaven's canopy
In lowering shadow and portentous gloom;
In pall of ambient obscurity.
The fork-ed lightnings ramify and play
Upon a background of sepulchral black;
The growling thunders rumble a reply
Of detonation awful and profound,
To every corruscation's vivid gleam;
In deep crescendo and fortissimo,
In quavering tremolo and stately fugue
Echoes, reverberates and dies away!

But soon the sun, with smiling radiance,
Through orifice, through rift and aperture,
Invades the storm, and dissipates the clouds,
Which scatter, cowering and ephemeral,
Hugging the cliffs, and o'er the dire abyss
Hover, in fleecy, ever changing form,
And in a transient season disappear;
Vanish, as man must vanish, and are gone.

The moist precipitation of the storm
Revives, refreshes and invigorates
The various vegetation, and bedews
Each blade of grass and floweret with a tear;
As nature, weeping o'er the faults of man.

The day recedes, and twilight's neutral shade
Succeeds in turn, and ushers in the night,
Whose wings, outstretched and shadowy, descend,
And in nocturnal mantle robes the scene.

A hush prevails! Oppressive and profound;
A silence, broken only by the breeze;
A dormant quiet-essence and repose;
Pervading calm and sweet oblivion,--
As nature wrapt in soft refreshing sleep.

Far in the east a solitary star
Peeps through the sombre curtain of the night--
In hesitating dubitation burns;
In lonely splendor, flashes for a time,
Till scattering celestial lights appear,--
The vanguard of an astral multitude
Of constellations, jewelled and serene,

Which fill the lofty dome of space, until
The heavens sparkle with the myriad
Of spectra, nebulae and satellite;
With stellar scintillation, and the orbs
Of less refulgence, which, reflective shine;
With falling star and trailing meteor;
In one grand culmination, glittering
To their Creator's glory!

A burst of mellow lunar radiance
Inundates and illuminates the scene;
The waxing moon, in her meridian full,
Her beam vicarious disseminates,
And shining, hides with her superior light,
The twinkling beauty of the firmament!

At the stupendous and inspiring sight
Of cosmic grandeur of the universe,
A sense of vague and overwhelming awe;
Of inconceivable immensity,
The being's inmost recess permeates;
And man, the atom in comparison,
In spellbound admiration, mutely stands;
With speculative meditation, dwells
On that most solemn of impressive thoughts,
The goodness of the Deity to man![1]

---

1   Composed at St. Anthony's hospital, Denver, Colo., from whence the author was led hopelessly blind.

# Nature's Child.

I love to tread the solitudes,
The forests and the trackless woods,
Where nature, undisturbed by man,
Pursues her voluntary plan.

Where nature's chemistry distills
The fountains and the laughing rills,
I love to quaff her sparkling wine,
And breathe the fragrance of the pine.

I love to dash the crystal dews
From floral shapes of varied hues,
And interweave the modest white
Of columbine in garlands bright.

I love to lie within the shade,
On grassy couch, by nature made,
And listen to the warbling notes
From her fair songsters' feathered throats.

And freed from artificial wants,
I love to dwell in nature's haunts,
And by the mountain's crystal lake
A rustic habitation make.

I love to scale the mountain height
And watch the eagle in his flight,
Or gaze upon the azure sea
Of aerial immensity.

I love the busy marts of trade,
I love the things which men have made,
Though man has charms, none such as these,
In him the child of nature sees.

## To the Pines.

Ye sad musicians of the wood,
Whose dirges fill the solitude,
Whose minor strains and melodies
Are wafted on the whispering breeze,
Whose plaintive chants and listless sighs,
Ascend as incense to the skies;
Do solemn tones afford relief,
With you, as men, a vent for grief?

## Reflections.

On the margin of a lakelet,
  In a rugged mountain clime,
Where precipice and pinnacle
  Of countenance sublime,
Cast their weird, austere reflections
  In the water's glistening sheen,
I strolled in contemplative mood,

Both pensive and serene.

As in a crystal mirror,
  In that lakelet's placid face,
I saw the mountains upside down,
  With all their pristine grace;
I saw each cliff and point of rocks,
  I saw the stately pine,
Inverted in fantastic form
  Below the water line.

I paused in admiration;
  And with calm complacency
I marveled at this photograph
  From nature's gallery;
And as my eyes surveyed the scene
  With solemn grandeur fraught,
This simile flashed through my mind
  As instantly as thought:

As the stern, majestic mountains,
  Without error or mistake,
Were reflected in the bosom
  Of that cool, pellucid lake,
So our every thought and action,
  Be it deed of hate or love,
May be photographed in record
  In that gallery above.

# Life's Mystery

I live, I move, I know not how, nor why,
  Float as a transient bubble on the air,
As fades the eventide I, too, must die;
  I came, I know not whence; I journey, where?

# The Fallen Tree.

I passed along a mountain road,
  Which led me through a wooded glen,
Remote from dwelling or abode
  And ordinary haunts of men;
    And wearied from the dust and heat.
    Beneath a tree, I found a seat.

The tree, a tall majestic spruce,
  Which had, perhaps for centuries,
Withstood, without a moment's truce,
  The wing-ed warfare of the breeze;
    A monarch of the solitude,
    Which well might grace the noblest wood.

Beneath its cool and welcome shade,
  Protected from the noontide rays,
The birds amid its branches played

And caroled forth their twittering praise;
  A squirrel perched upon a limb
  And chattered with loquacious vim.

E'er yet that selfsame week had sped,
  On my return, I sought its shade;
But where it reared its form, instead;
  A fallen monarch I surveyed,
    Prostrate and broken on the ground,
    Nor longer cast its shade around.

Uprooted and disheveled, there
  The monarch of the forest lay;
As if in desolate despair
  Its last resistance fell away,
    And overwhelmed, in evil hour
    Went down before the tempest's power.

Such are the final works of fate;
  The birds to other branches flew;
And man, whatever his estate,
  Must face that same mutation, too!
    To-day, I stand erect and tall,
    The morrow--may record my fall.

# There is an Air of Majesty.

There is an air of majesty,
A bearing dignified and free,
   About the mountain peaks;
Each crag of weather-beaten stone
Presents a grandeur of its own
   To him who seeks.

There is a proud, defiant mein,
Expressive, stern, and yet serene,
   About the precipice;
Whose rugged form looks grimly down,
And answers, with an austere frown
   The sunlight's kiss.

The mountain, with the snow bank crowned;
The gorge, abysmal and profound;
   Impress with aspect grand:
With unfeigned reverence I see
In canon and declivity
   The All-Wise Hand.

# Think Not that the Heart is Devoid of Emotion.

Think not that the heart is devoid of emotion,
  Because of a countenance rugged and stern,
The bosom may hide the most fervent devotion,
  As shadowy forests hide floweret and fern;
As the pearls which are down in the depths of the ocean,
  The heart may have treasures which few can discern.

Think not the heart barren, because no reflection
  Is flashed from the depths of its secret embrace;
External appearance may baffle detection,
  And yet the heart beat with an ethical grace:
The breast may be charged with the truest affection
  And never betray it by action or face.

# Humanity's Stream.

I stood upon a crowded thoroughfare,
Within a city's confines, where were met
All classes and conditions, and surveyed,
From a secluded niche or aperture,
The various, ever-changing multitude
Which passed along in restless turbulence,
And, as a human river, ebbed and flowed
Within its banks of brick and masonry.

Within this vast and heterogeneous throng,
One might discern all stages and degrees,
From wealth and power to helpless indigence;
Extravagance to trenchant penury,
And all extremes of want and misery.
Some blest by wealth, some cursed by poverty;
Some in positions neutral to them both;
Some wore a gaunt and ill-conditioned look
Which told its tale of lack of nourishment;
While others showed that irritated air
Which speaks of gout and pampered appetite;
Some following vocations quite reverse
From those which nature had endowed them for;
Some passed with face self-satisfied and calm,
As if the world bore nothing else but joy;
And some there were who, from the cradle's mouth,
As they pursued their journey to the grave,
Had felt no throb save that of misery;
The man of large affairs passed by in haste,
With mind preoccupied, nor thought of else
Save undertakings which concerned himself;
The shallow son of misplaced opulence
Came strutting by with self-important air,
With head erect in a contemptuous poise,
As if the stars were subject to his will,
And e'en the golden sun was something base,
Which had offended with its wholesome light
In shining on so great a personage,
A being more than ordinary clay,
And much superior to the vulgar herd!
Some faces passed which knew no kindly look,
And felt no friendly pressure of the hand;
And if the face depict the character,

Some passed so steeped in crime and villainy
That Judas' vile, ill-favored countenance
Would seem in contrast quite respectable;
Some features glowed with unfeigned honesty,
Some grimaced in dissimulating craft,
Some smiled benignantly and passed along;
Some faces meek, some stern and resolute;
Some the embodiment of gentleness;
Some whose specific aspects plainly told
Their fondest dreams were not of earth, but heaven;
A newly wedded couple passed that way,
In the sweet zenith of their honeymoon,
But little dreaming what the future held.
The light and trivial fool, the brainless fop;
The staid and sober priest and minister;
And she who worshiped at proud fashion's shrine;
The mental giant, serious and sad;
The thoughtful student and philosopher;
And some of intellect diminutive;
The man of letters, with abstracted mien,
And he whose every thought was on the toil
Which made his bare existence possible;
The blushing maiden, pure and innocent;
The stately grandam, dignified and gray;
The matron, with the babe upon her breast;
The silly superannuated flirt,
Who nursed her waning beauty day by day,
And still essayed to act the role of youth;
The gay coquette and belle of other days,
Who in life's morning, with disdainful laugh,
Had quaffed the cup of pleasure to its dregs,
And now, grown old, must pay the penalty
In wrinkles and uncourted loneliness;

The widow, who, but newly desolate,
Would grasp a hand, then start to find it gone;
The spendthrift and the sordid usurer,
Who knew no sentiment save lust for gold;
The bloated drunkard, sinking 'neath the weight
Of wassail inclination dissolute;
The youth, who, following his baleful steps,
Reeled for the first time from intemperance;
And she who had forgot her covenant,
In brazen infamy and unwept shame;--
The good, the bad, the impious and unjust,
The energetic and the indolent,
The adolescent and the venerable,
Passed by, pursuant of their various ways.

*       *       *       *       *

The aged and decrepit plodded by,
Whom one would think were ripe for any tomb,
Yet quailed at dissolution's very thought;
The crippled and deformed, with cane and crutch,
Came limping by, as eddies in the stream;
The mendicant, whose eyes might never see
The golden sunlight, felt his way along,
And though the world was dark, still shrank from death.
Some faces showed the trace of recent tears,
And some revealed the impress of despair;
Others endeavored with a careless smile
To hide a breast surcharged with hopelessness,
As one afflicted with a foul disease
Strives to avoid the scrutinizing gaze
By the assumption of indifference;
Some whose misfortunes and adversities

And oft repeated disappointments, dried
The fountain heads of kindness, and had turned
Life's sweetest joys to gall and bitterness.
Each face betrayed some sort or form of woe;
In more than one I read a tragedy.

\*       \*       \*       \*       \*

How complex is existence! What a maze
Of complication and entanglement!
Each thread combining with the other threads
Fulfills its office in the labyrinth;
Each link concatenates the other links
Which constitute the vast and endless chain
Of human life, and human destiny,--
The strange phantasmagoria of fate.

\*       \*       \*       \*       \*

So we, in life's procession, pass along
To the accompaniment of secret dirge,
Or laughter interspersed with tear and groan;
Nor pause a moment, nor retrace a step,
But march in Fate's spectacular review
In pageant to our common goal--
                    The Grave.

# Nature's Lullaby.

A MOUNTAIN NOCTURNE

In forest shade my couch is made.
  And there I calmly lie,
With thought confined in pensive mind,
  And contemplate the sky;
I wonder if the frowning cliff,
  The valley and the wood,
Or rugged freaks of mountain peaks,
  Enjoy their solitude.

The heavens hold a sphere of gold,
  A full and placid moon,
Suspended high, in cloudless sky,
  With constellations strewn;
Its mellow beam, on rill and stream,
  In silvery sheen I see;
Before its light, the shades of night
  As evil spirits, flee.

In space afar, a shooting star,
  With swift, uncertain course,
In dazzling sparks its passage marks,
  As it expends its force;
The mountains bare reflect its glare
  Of weird, unearthly light,
And e'en the skies, in glad surprise,
  Behold its gorgeous flight.

The spruce and pine, at timber-line,
  In straggling patches strewn,
Surcharge the breeze with melodies,
  The forests' plaintive tune;
As they descend, the waters blend
  In babbling harmony,
And soothe to rest my tranquil breast,
  With Nature's lullaby.

# The Spirit of freedom is Born of the Mountains.

The spirit of freedom is born of the mountains,
In gorge and in canon it hovers and dwells;
Pervading the torrents and crystalline fountains,
  Which dash through the valleys and forest clad dells.

The spirit of freedom, so firm and impliant,
  Is borne on the breeze, whose invisible waves
Descend from the mountain peaks, stern and defiant--
  Created for freemen, but never for slaves.

# The Valley of the San Miguel.

In the golden West, by fond Nature blest,
  Lies a vale which my heart holds dear;
Where the zephyr blows from eternal snows
  And tempers the atmosphere;
Where the torrent falls o'er the mountain walls,
  As its thunderous echoes thrill,
Where the sparkling mist, by the rainbow kissed,
  Decks the Valley of San Miguel[2].

Where the birds of spring, in their season sing,
  Their spontaneous melodies;
Where the columbine and the stately pine
  Stand quivering in the breeze;
Where the aspen tall hugs the trachyte wall,
  And the wild rose bedecks the hill;
Where the willows weep, and their vigils keep,
  On the banks of the San Miguel.

Where the mountains high, cleave the azure sky,
  With their turrets so bleak and gray;
Where the morning light crowns the dizzy height,
  At the break of the summer's day;
Where the crags look down with an austere frown,
  O'er the valley so calm and still;
Where the mesas blue, blend their dreamy hue
  With the skies of the San Miguel.

Where the mountains hold a vast wealth of gold,

---

2  San Miguel, pronounced "Magill," the Spanish form of St. Michael.

In the quartz ledge and placer bar;
Where the hills resound with the constant sound
  Of the stamp mill's battering jar;
Where the waters dash with the rhythmic splash
  Of the cascade and mountain rill,
As they laugh and flow to the lands below,
  Through the turbulent San Miguel.

Where the shadows glide, in the eventide,
  As the sun, to nocturnal rest,
With the dazzling rays of a world ablaze,
  Sinks into the distant west;
When the yellow leaf of existence brief,
  Brings the hour when the pulse is still,
May my ashes rest in the golden West,
  On the banks of the San Miguel.

# To Mother Huberta.

As repeated in chorus on the anniversary of her Names-day by the
Sisters of St. Hubert at St. Anthony's Hospital, Denver, Col., Oct. 29,
1900.

Mother, our greetings be to thee,
On the glad anniversary
  Of this, thy festive day;
Thy daughters, daughters not of earth,
But bound by cords of Heavenly birth,
  Their love and greetings pay.

We thank thee, Mother, for thy care,
Thy watchfulness, and fervent prayer;
  And if 'tis Heaven's will,
May many a returning year
And namesday find our Mother here,
  Constant and watchful still.

Blest be that autumn brown and sere!
Bless-ed the day and blest the year,
  Of his[3] nativity!
Blest be the hospitals, which rise,
Resultant of thy enterprise,
  Thy zeal and fervency.

Blest be that hunter[4] saint of thine!
Bless-ed the deer, and blest the sign
  Between its antlers broad!
To us, thy daughters, is it given
To bless thee, in the name of Heaven,
  And blessing thee, bless God.

---

3   St. Hubert.
4   St. Hubert, the apostle of Ardennes, a saint of the Roman Catholic Church, the patron of hunts-men. He was of a noble family of Acquitaine. While hunting in the forests of Ardennes he had a vision of a stag with a shining crucifix between its antlers, and heard a warning voice. He was converted, entered the church, and eventually became Bishop of Maestricht and Liege. He worked many miracles, and is said to have died in 727 or 729. Spofford's Cyclopaedia, Vol. 4, page 470.

# Suggested by a Mountain Eagle.

I gazed at the azure-hued mantle of heaven,
  The measureless depths of ethereal space;
I gazed at the clouds, so invisibly driven,
  And an eagle, which wheeled with symmetrical grace.

I gazed at that eagle, majestically wheeling,
  With dignity, born of the free mountain air;
I envied that bird, with an envious feeling
  Which springs from a heart that is shackled with care.

I envied that eagle, which bowed to no master,
  But soared at his will, through the ambient skies,
Defiant of danger, and scorning disaster,
  He screamed at the cliffs, which re-echoed his cries.

I envied that bird, on that fair summer morning,
  When nature lay decked with spontaneous art,
As he circled, with aspect defiant and scorning,
  And perched on a pinnacle's loftiest part.


And scanning the scene with a stern indecision,
He spread his dark wings, with intuitive cries,
And sped, till acute and inquisitive vision
  Discerned but a movable speck in the skies.

When the shades of the evening, so listless and dreary,
  Descend on the valley, his wing never flags,
As through the dark shadows he soars to his eyerie,

Which nestles among the impregnable crags.

Ah! fain would I rise on thy feathery pinions,
  Above the material cares of the day,
And float over earth's most enchanting dominions,
  As clouds, by the zephyrs, are wafted away!

# The Silvery San Juan.

Wherever I wander, my spirit still dwells,
In the silvery San Juan[5] with its streamlet and dells;
Whose mountainous summits, so rugged and high,
With their pinnacles pierce the ethereal sky;
Where the daisy, the rose, and the sweet columbine
Blend their colors with those of the sober hued pine;
Where the ceaseless erosions of measureless time,
Have chiseled the grotto and canon sublime;
Have sculptured the cliff, and the stern mountain wall;
Have formed the bold turret, impressive and tall;
Have cut the deep gorge with its wonderful caves,
Sepulchral and gloomy; whose vast architraves
Support the stalactites, both pendant and white,
Which with the stalagmites beneath them unite;
Where nestles a valley, sequestered and grand,
Worn out of the rock by the same tireless hand,
Surrounded by mountains, majestic and gray,
Which smile from their heights on the Town of Ouray.

---

5   Pronounced San Wan. Spanish form of St. John.

*   *   *   *

Wherever I wander, my ears hear the sound
Of thy waters, which plunge with a turbulent bound
O'er the precipice, seething and laden with foam;
My ears hear their music wherever I roam;
Where the cataract's rhapsody, joyous and light,
Enchants in the morning and soothes in the night;
Where blend the loud thunders, sonorous and deep,
With the sobs of the rain as the black heavens weep;
Where the whispering zephyr, and murmuring breeze,
Unite with the soft, listless sigh of the trees;
And where to the fancy, the voices of air
Wail in tones of distress, or in shrieks of despair;
Where mourneth the night wind, with desolate breath,
In accents suggestive of sorrow and death;
As falls from the heavens, so fleecy and light,
The winter's immaculate mantle of white;
Wherever I wander, these sounds greet my ears,
And the silvery San Juan to my fancy appears.

# As the Shifting Sands of the Desert.

As the shifting sands of the desert
  Are born by the simoon's wrath,
And in wanton and fleet confusion,
  Are strewn on its trackless path;

So our lives with resistless fury,
  Insensibly and unknown,
With a restless vacillation
  By the winds of fate are blown;
    But an All-Wise Hand
    May have changed the sand,
    For a purpose of His own.


As the troubled and turbulent waters,
  As the waves of the angry main,
Respond with their undulations
  To the breath of the hurricane;
So our lives on Time's boundless ocean
  Unwittingly toss and roll,
And unconsciously drift with the current
  Which evades our assumed control;
    But a Hand of love,
    From the skies above,
    May have guided us past a shoal.


Ephemeral, mobile, and fleeting,
  Our delible paths we tread;
And fade as the crimson sunset,
  When the heavens are tinged with red;
As the gorgeously tinted rainbow
  Retains not its varied dyes,
  We change, with the constant mutation,
  Of desert, of sea, and skies;
    But the Hand which made,
    Knows each transient shade,
  Which passes before the eyes.

# Missed.

Pity the child who never feels
  A mother's fond caress;
That childish smile a void conceals
  Of aching loneliness.

Pity the heart which loves in vain,
  What balm or mystic spell
Can soothe that bosom's secret pain,
  The pain it may not tell?

Pity those missed by Cupid's darts,
  For 'twas ordained for such,
Who love at random, but whose hearts
  Feel no responsive touch.

# If I Have Lived Before.

If I have lived before, some evidence
  Should that existence to the present bind;
Some innate inkling of experience
  Should still imbue and permeate the mind,
If we, progressing, pass from state to state,
Or retrograde, as turns the wheel of fate.

If I have lived before, and could my eyes
  But view the scenes wherein that life was spent,
Or even for an instant recognize
  The climes, conditions and environment
Beloved by them in that pre-natal span,
Though past and future both be sealed to man;

Or, if perchance, kind memory should ope'
  Her floodgates, with fond recollection fraught,
'Twould then renew the dormant fires of hope,
  Now smothered out by speculative thought;
'Twould then rekindle faith within a breast,
Where doubt is now the sole remaining guest.

## The Darker Side.

They say that all nature is smiling and gay,
  And the birds the most happy of all,
But the sparrow, pursued by the sparrowhawk,
  Savors more of the wormwood and gall.

They say that all nature is smiling and gay,
  But the groan may dissemble the laugh;
E'en now from the meadow is wafted the sound
  Of a bovine bewailing her calf.

They say that all nature is smiling and gay,
  But the moss often covers the rock;
Every animal form is beset by a foe,

For the wolf always follows the flock.

For the animal holds all inferior flesh
  As its just and legitimate prey;
Every scream of the eagle a panic creates
  As the weaker things scamper away.

They say that all nature is smiling and gay,
  But the smiles are all needed to sweeten
The struggle we see so incessantly waged
  To eat, and avoid being eaten.

And men, with their genial competitive ways
  Present no decided improvements,
For their personal gain they will sacrifice all
  Who may stand in the way of their movements.

# The Miner.

    Clink! Clink! Clink!
  The song of the hammer and drill!
At the sound of the whistle so shrill and clear,
He must leave the wife and the children dear,
  In his cabin upon the hill.
    Clink! Clink! Clink!
But the arms that deliver the sturdy stroke,
Ere the shift is done, may be crushed or broke,
Or the life may succumb to the gas and smoke,
  Which the underground caverns fill.

Clink! Clink! Clink!
 The song of the hammer and drill!
As he toils in the shaft, in the stope or raise,
'Mid dangers which lurk, but elude the gaze,
 His nerves with no terrors thrill.
 Clink! Clink! Clink!
For the heart of the miner is strong and brave;
Though the rocks may fall, and the shaft may cave
And become his dungeon, if not his grave,
 He braves every thought of ill.

 Clink! Clink! Clink!
 The song of the hammer and drill!
But the heart which is beating in unison
With the steady stroke, e'er the shift is done,
 May be cold and forever still.
 Clink! Clink! Clink!
He may reap the harvest of danger sowed,
The hole which he drills he may never load,
For the powder may e'en in his hand explode,
 To mangle, if not to kill.

 Clink! Clink! Clink!
 The song of the hammer and drill!
Facing dangers more grim than the cannon's mouth;
Breathing poisons more foul than the swamps of the south
 In their tropical fens distill.
 Clink! Clink! Clink!
Thus the battle he fights for his daily bread;
Thus our gold and our silver, our iron and lead,
Cost us lives, as true as our blood is red,
 And probably always will.

# Life's Undercurrent.

Within the precincts of a hospital,
　I wandered in a sympathetic mood;
Where face to face with wormwood and with gall,
　With wrecks of pain and stern vicissitude,
The eye unused to human misery
Might view life's undercurrent vividly.

My gaze soon rested on the stricken form
　Of one succumbing to the fever's drouth,
With throbbing brow intolerably warm,
　With wasted lips and mute appealing mouth;
And when I watched that prostrate figure there
I thought that fate must be the worst to bear.

I next beheld a thin but patient face,
　Aged by the constant twinge of hopeless pain,
Wheeled in an easy chair from place to place,
　A form which ne'er might stand erect again;
I viewed that human shipwreck in his chair,
And thought a fate like that was worst to bear.

Within her room a beauteous maiden lay,
　Moaning in agony no words express,
A cancer eating rapidly away
　Her vital force,--so foul and pitiless;
And when I saw that face, so young and fair,
I thought such anguish was the worst to bear.

A helpless paralytic met my eyes,

Whose hands might never grasp a friendly hand,
But hung distorted and of shrunken size,
  Insensible to muscular command;
His face an abject picture of despair;
I thought a fate like that was worst to bear.

With wasted form, emaciate and wan,
  A pale consumptive coughed with labored breath,
His sunken eyes and hectic flush upon
  His cheek, foretold a sure but lingering death;
I thought, whene'er I met his hollow stare,
A wasting death like that was worst to bear.

That day with fetters obdurate and fast,
  With chain of summer, winter, spring and fall,
Is bounden to the dim receding past;
  Time o'er my life has spread a somber pall,
With sightless eyes I grope and clutch the air,
My lot is now the hardest lot to bear.

# They Cannot See the Wreaths We Place.

They cannot see the wreaths we place
  Upon the silent bier,
They cannot see the tear-stained face,
  Nor feel the scalding tear,
And now can flowers or graven stone,
For wrongs done them in life atone?

Better the flower that smooths the thorns
  On earthly pathway found,
Than that which uselessly adorns
  The bier or silent mound.
And neither tear nor floral token
Retracts the hasty word, when spoken.

Then strew the flowers ere life has fled,
  While yet their eyes discern;
Why waste their fragrance on the dead
  Who no fond smile return?
The heaving breast with sorrow aches,
Comfort the throbbing heart which breaks.


# Mother.--Alpha and Omega.


Mother! Mother!
  The startled cry of childish fright
  Rang through the silence of the night,
  As but the mother's fond caress
  Could soothe its infantile distress;
  And the mother answered, with loving stroke
  Of her gentle hand, as she softly spoke:
  "Hush, hush, my child, that troubled cry;
  What evil can harm thee, with mother nigh?"

Mother! Mother!
  Long years have passed, and the fevered brow
  Of a bearded man, she is stroking now,

As through delirium and pain
He cries as a little child, again.
And the mother answered, with loving stroke
Of her careworn hand, as she softly spoke:
"Hush, hush, my child, that troubled cry;
What evil can harm thee, with mother nigh?"

Mother! Mother!
Still time rolls on, and an old man stands
Trembling on life's declining sands;
As memory bridges the flood of years
He cries as a child, with childish tears;
And memory answers, with loving stroke
Of a vanished hand, and an echo spoke:
"Hush, hush, my child, that troubled cry;
What evil can harm thee, with mother nigh?"


# Empty are the Mother's Arms.


Ah, empty are the mother's arms
   Which clasp a vanished form;
A darling spared from life's alarms,
   And safe from earthly storm.

In absent reverie, she hears
   That voice, nor can forget;
The fond illusion disappears,--
   Her arms are empty, yet.

# In Deo Fides.

Almighty God! Supreme! Most High!
  Before Thy throne, in reverence, we kneel;
We cannot realize Thine infinity;
  Beholding not, we can Thy presence feel;
Though veiled impenetrably, Thou dost reveal
Such evidence as clouds cannot conceal!

Acknowledged, though unseen, Almighty Power!
  Within its secret depths, the bosom pays
In pleasure's or affliction's calmer hour,
  The heart's sincerest offering of praise;
Intuitive, unuttered prayers arise
Without the outstretched arms, or reverently clos-ed eyes.

Down deep within the soul's mysterious seat,
  The voice of reason, and inherent sense,
Admits Thy Sovereign Power, and doth entreat
  The guidance of a Just Omnipotence;
Thus doth the human essence e'er depend
On that Supreme. Eternal. Without End.

Supreme, Mysterious Power! Whate'er Thou be,
  Can e'er our mortal natures comprehend,
This side the veil which shrouds futurity,
  Thy Wisdom, Power, and Love? The end
Of all conclusions, reasoned o'er and o'er,
We know Thou dost exist! Can we know more?

# Shall Love, as the Bridal Wreath, Whither and Die?

Shall love as the bridal wreath, wither and die?
  Or remain ever constant and sure,
As the years of the future pass rapidly by,
And the waves of adversity's tempest roll high,
  Ever changeless and fervent endure?

Mistake not the fancy, that lasts but a day,
  For the love which eternally thrives;
That sentiment false, is as prone to decay
As the wreath is to fade and to wither away;
  And like it, it never revives.

# Shall Our Memories Live When the Sod Rolls Above Us?

Shall our memories live, when the sod rolls above us
  And marks our last home with a mouldering heap?
Shall the voices of those who profess that they love us
  E'er mention our names, as we dreamlessly sleep?

Will their eyes ever dim at some fond recollection,
  Or their hands ever plant a small flower o'er the breast,
Or will they gaze with a sad circumspection
  At the tablets, which tell of our last solemn rest?

Ah! soon shall the hearts which our memories cherish
  Forget, as they strive with the cares of their own;
And even the last dim remembrance shall perish
  As we peacefully slumber, unwept and unknown.

But if our lives, though of transient duration,
  Are filled with some work in humanity's name,
Some uplifting effort, or self-immolation,
  Our memories shall live in the temples of Fame.


# A Reverie.


O, tomb of the past
Where buried hopes lie,
In my visions I see
Thy phantoms pass by!
A form, long departed,
  Before me appears;
A sweet voice, long silent,
  Again greets my ears.

Fond memory dwells
  On the things that have been;
And my eyes calmly gaze
  On a long vanished scene;
A scene such as memory
  Stores deep in the breast,
Which only appears
  In a season of rest.

Once more we wander,
  Her fair hand in mine;
Once more her promise,
  "I'll ever be thine";
Once more the parting,
  The shroud, and the pall,
The sods' hollow thump
  As they coffinward fall.

The reverie ends--
  All the fancies have flown;
And my sad, lonely heart,
  Now seems doubly alone;
As the Ivy, whose tendrils
  Reach longingly out,
Yet finds not an oak
  To entwine them about.

# Love's Plea.

I love thee, my darling, both now and forever,
  My heart feels the thralldom of love's mystic spell,
'Tis fettered with shackles which nothing can sever,
  To the heart which responds to its passionate swell.

I love thee, my darling, with love that is stronger,
  Than all the fond ties which the heart holds enshrined;
Adversity, sorrow or pain can no longer
  Detract from this heart, if with thine intertwined.

I love thee, my darling, with sacred affection,
  Which death, nor the cycles of time shall efface;
Nor from my heart's mirror, erase thy reflection,
  Nor tear thy fond heart from its fervent embrace.

# Ashes to Ashes, Dust to Dust.

Is there a Death? The light of day
At eventide shall fade away;
From out the sod's eternal gloom
The flowers, in their season, bloom;
Bud, bloom and fade, and soon the spot
Whereon they flourished knows them not;
Blighted by chill, autumnal frost;
"Ashes to ashes, dust to dust!"

Is there a Death? Pale forms of men
To formless clay resolve again;
Sarcophagus of graven stone,
Nor solitary grave, unknown,
Mausoleum, or funeral urn,
No answer to our cries return;
Nor silent lips disclose their trust;
"Ashes to ashes, dust to dust!"

Is there a Death? All forms of clay
Successively shall pass away;
But, as the joyous days of spring
Witness the glad awakening

Of nature's forces, may not men,
In some due season, rise again?
Then why this calm, inherent trust,
"If ashes to ashes, dust to dust?"

# Despair.

Ill fares the heart, when hope has fled;
   When vanishes each prospect fair,
When the last flickering ray has sped,
   And naught remains but mute despair;
When inky blackness doth enshroud
   The hopes the heart once held in store,
As some tall pine, by great winds bowed,
   Doth snap, and when the tempest's o'er,
Its noble form, magnificent and proud,
   Doth prostrate lie, nor ever riseth more;
   Thus breaks the heart, which sees no hope before.

Ill fares the heart, when hope has fled;
   That heart is as some ruin old,
With ancient arch and wall, o'erspread
   With moss, and desolating mold;
Whose banquet halls, where once the sound
   Of revelry rang unconfined,
Now, with the hoot of owls resound,
   Or echo back the mournful wind;
In whose foul nooks the gruesome bat is found.
   The heart a ruin is, when unresigned;

No hope before, and but regret behind.

Ill fares the heart, when hope has fled;
  That heart, to fate unreconciled,
Though throbbing, is as truly dead
  As though by foul decay defiled;
That heart is as a grinning skull,
  With smiling mockery, and stare
Of eyeless sockets, or the hull
  Of shipwrecked vessel, bleached and bare,
Derelict, morbid, apathetic, dull,
  As drowning men, who clutch the empty air,
  The heart goes down, which feels but blind despair.

# Hidden Sorrows.

For some the river of life would seem
  Free from the shallow, the reef, or bar,
As they gently glide down the silvery stream
  With scarcely a ripple, a lurch, or jar;
But under the surface, calm and fair,
  Lurk the hidden snags, and the secret care;
The waters are deepest where still, and clear,
And the sternest anguish forbids a tear.

For others, the pathway of life is strewn
  With many a thorn, for each rose or bud;
And their journey o'er mountain, o'er moor, and dune,
  Can be plainly tracked by footprints of blood;

But deeper still lies the hidden smart
　Of some secret sorrow, which gnaws the heart,
And rankles under a surface clear;
For the sternest anguish forbids a tear.

But, when the journey's end we see,
　At the bar of the Judge of quick and dead,
The cross, which the one bore silently
May outweigh his of the bloodstained tread.
The cross unseen, and the cross of light,
　May balance in that Judge's sight;
O'er the heart that is breaking a smile may appear,
For the sternest anguish forbids a tear.

# O, a Beautiful Thing Is the Flower That Fadeth!

O, a beautiful thing is the flower that fadeth,
　And perishing, smiles on the chill autumn wind;
A sweet desolation its ruin pervadeth,
　A fragrant remembrance still lingers behind.

O, a beautiful thing is the glad consummation
　Of a life that is upright, untarnished and pure;
That spirit, when freed from this earth's animation,
　Shall live, as the heavens eternal endure!

# Smiles.

There is the warm, congenial smile,
  Benign, and honest, too,
Free from deception, fraud, and guile;
  The smile of friendship true.

There is the smile most fair to see,
Which wreathes the modest glance
Of spotless maiden purity;
  The smile of innocence.

There is the smile of woman's love,
  That potent, siren spell,
Which uplifts men to heaven above,
  Or lures them down to hell!

There is the vain, derisive smile,
  Of cynical conceit;
The drunken leer, the grimace vile,
  Of lives with crime replete.

There is the smile of vacancy,
  Expressionless, we find
On idiot physiognomy,
  The vacuum of a mind.

There is a smile, which more than tears
  Or language can express;
The grim disguise which anguish wears,
  The mask of dire distress

There is a smile of practiced art,
  More false than treason's kiss;
But penetrate that dual heart,
  And hear the serpent's hiss.

A smile, the visage shall embrace,
  When nature's cup is full;
Behind the stern and frowning face
  There lies a grinning skull.


# A Request.


When close by my bed the Death Angel shall stand
  And deliver his summons, at last;
When my brow feels the chill of his cold, clammy hand,
  And mortality's struggles are past;
When my pain throbbing temples, with death sweat are cold,
  And the spirit its strivings shall cease,
As with muscular shrug, it relaxes its hold,
  And the suffering clay is at peace;

E'er my spirit shall plunge through the shadowy vale,
  My lips shall this wish have expressed,
That all which remains of mortality frail,
  In some fair enclosure may rest;
Where disorganized, this pale form shall sustain
  The fragrant and beautiful flowers,
And reproduce beauty, again and again,
  Through nature's grand organic powers.

# Battle Hymn.

Almighty Power! Who through the past
  Our Nation's course has safely led;
Behold again the sky o'ercast,
  Again is heard the martial tread!
    Our stay in each contingency,
    Our Father's God, we turn to thee!

For lo! The bugle note of war
  Is wafted from a southern strand!
O Lord of Battles! we implore
  The guidance of Thy mighty hand,
    While as of yore, the hero draws
    His sword in Freedom's sacred cause!

And when at last the oaken wreath
  Shall crown afresh the victor's brow;
And Peace the conquering sword resheath,
  Be with us then, as well as now!
    Our stay in each contingency,
    In peace or war, we turn to Thee!

# The Nations Peril.

Ill fares the land, to hastening ills a prey,
Where wealth accumulates and men decay.
--Goldsmith.


I fear the palace of the rich,
  I fear the hovel of the poor;
Though fortified by moat and ditch,
  The castle strong could not endure;
Nor can the squalid hovel be
  A source of strength, and those who cause
This widening discrepancy
  Infringe on God's eternal laws.

The heritage of man, the earth,
  Was framed for homes, not vast estates;
A lowering scale of human worth
  Each generation demonstrates,
Which feels the landlord's iron hand,
  And hopeless, plod with effort brave;
Who love no home can love no land;
  These own no home, until the grave.

The nation's strongest safeguards lie
In free and unencumbered homes;
Not in its hordes of vagrancy,
Nor in its proud, palatial domes;
Nor can the mercenary sword
  E'er cross with that the freeman draws.

Nor oil upon the waters poured
  Perpetuate an unjust cause.

Eternal Justice, still prevail
  And stay this menace ere too late!
Ere sturdy manhood droop and fail,
  The law, immutable, of fate;
No foe can daunt the stalwart heart
  Of him who guards that sacred ground
Where every hero owns a part,
  Where each an ample home has found.

No more shall battle's lurid gleam
  The cloudless sky of peace obscure;
Nor blood becrimson field, or stream,
  Nor avarice grind down the poor;
But onward let thy progress be
  A pageant, beautiful and grand;
May He who e'er has guided thee
  Protect thee still, my native land!

# Echoes from Galilee.

What means this gathering multitude,
  Upon thy shores, O, Galilee,
As various as the billows rude
  That sweep thy ever restless sea?
    Can but the mandate of a King
    So varied an assemblage bring?

Behold the noble, rich, and great,
  From Levite, Pharisee and Priest,
Down to the lowest dregs of fate,
  From mightiest even to the least;
    Yes, in this motley throng we find
    The palsied, sick, mute, halt, and blind.

Is this some grand affair of state,
  A coronation, or display,
By some vainglorious potentate,--
  Or can this concourse mark the day
    Of some victorious hero's march
    Homeward, through triumphal arch?

Or, have they come to celebrate
  Some sacred sacerdotal rite;
By civic feast, to emulate
Some deed, on history's pages bright?
    Or can this grand occasion be
    Some battle's anniversary?

But wherefore come the halt and blind?

What comfort can the pain-distressed
In such a tumult hope to find?
  What is there here, to offer rest
    To those, whom adverse fate has hurled,
    Dismantled, on a hostile world?

Let us approach! A form we see,
  Fairest beyond comparison;
For such an heavenly purity,
  From other eyes, hath never shown;
    Nor such a calm, majestic brow
    On earth hath ne'er appeared, till now.

Draw nearer. Lo! a voice we hear,
  Resonant, soft, pathetic, sweet;
In ringing accents, calm and clear,
  He sways the thousands at his feet,
    With more than mortal eloquence,
    Or man's compassion, in his glance.

Ah! Strange, that such a form should stand
  In raiment soiled, and travel stained;
Yes, mark the contour of that hand,
  A hand by menial toil profaned.
Can one from such a station reach
    All classes by sheer force of speech?

Can eloquence from mortal tongue
  Break through the barriers, which divide
The toiling and down-trodden throng
  From affluence, and official pride?
    Then how can yonder speaker hold
    An audience so manifold?

He spake as never orator
  Before, or since, with burning thought,
In parable, and metaphor;
  Each simple illustration taught
    Some sacred truth, some truth which could
    By sage, or fool, be understood.

With similes of common things,
  The lilies of the field, the salt
Which lost its savour; gently brings
  A lesson, from the common fault
    Of self-admiring Pharisee,
    Of ostentatious piety.

And from the prostrate penitent,
  The Publican, who beat his breast,
Remorsefully his garment rent,
  And thus, with tears, his sin confessed;
"Lord, Lord, a sinner vile am I,
    Be merciful, and hear my cry!"

And from that man, beset by thieves,
  And left upon the road, to die;
No aid or comfort he receives
  From Priest, or Levite, passing by;
    How the despised Samaritan
    Proved the true neighbor to that man.

Yes, finished with such fervency
  Of gesture, and similitude;
Such depths of love, and purity
  His hearers marvelled, as they stood;
    Nor through his discourse, was there heard,

Abusive, vain, or idle word.

Who may this wondrous speaker be?
  Is he some judge, or orator?
Some one in high authority?
  Physician, prince, or conqueror?
    Answer, thou ever restless sea,
    Who may this wondrous person be?

With echoes soft, the sea replies,
  This is a Judge, and Orator;
A Judge, beyond all judges wise,
  And eloquent, as none before;
A Judge, majestic, calm, serene;
  And yet, an humble Nazarene.

He is a Ruler, whose command
  The myriads of the skies obey,
As in the hollow of His hand
  He holds all human destiny.
    The tempest wild concedes his will,
    And calms before His "Peace, be still."

A great Physician, too, is He,
  Whose word, the leper purifies;
The mute converse, the blind ones see;
  At his command, the dead arise;
    He cures the ravages of sin,
    And makes the foulest sinner clean.

He is a Prince, a Prince whose power
  Knows neither limit nor degree,
Whose glory, not the passing hour,

Nor cycles of futurity,
　Can augment, alter, or decrease--
　Prince is He, the Prince of Peace.

He is earth's greatest Conqueror,
　But conquers not with crimson sword;
Love is the weapon of His war,
　Forgiveness, and gentle word;
　But, greatest of all victories,
　O'er the dark grave, His banner flies.

## Go, And Sin No More.

When the poor, erring woman sought
　In tears the Master's feet,
Her breast, with deep contrition fraught,
　Repentance, full, complete,
Divine compassion filled His eyes,
　He spake, says Sacred Lore,--
"O, erring heart, forgiven, rise,
　Go, thou, and sin no more."

The tear of contrite sorrow, shed
　By penitence, cast down,
Shall flash, when solar rays have fled,
　In an eternal crown;
That tear shall scintillate, and shine,
　When comets cease to soar;
If thou would'st wear that gem divine,
Go, thou, and sin no more!

# Gently Lead Me, Star Divine.

Gently lead me, Star Divine,
  Lead with bright unchanging ray;
O'er my lowly pathway shine,
  I shall never lose my way;
Though uncertain be my tread,
Pitfalls deep, and mountains high,
  Safely shall my feet be led,
    By Thy beacon, in the sky.

Long ago, while journeying
  Westward, o'er the desert wild,
Sages sought a promised King
  In the person of a child;
By Thy bright illuminings,
  To that manger, in the fold,
Thou did'st lead those shepherd kings;
  Lead me, as Thou lead'st of old.

# Dying Hymn.

The hour-glass speeds its final sands,
  In splendor sinks the golden sun,
So men must yield to death's demands
  When human life its course has run.

We view the ruins of the past,
  We stand surrounded by decay,
Our transient hours are speeding fast
  And, e'er we think, have passed away.

Weep not, nor mourn with idle tear
That hour, inevitable and sure;
  We move, our sojourn finished here,
    To nobler realms which shall endure.

## In Mortem Meditare.

## DYING THOUGHTS.

As Life's receding sunset fades
    And night descends,
I calmly watch the gathering shades,
As darkness stealthily invades
    And daylight ends.

Earth's span is drawing to its close,
    With every breath;
My pain-racked brain no respite knows,
Yet shrinks it, from the grim repose
    It feels in death.

The curtain falls on Life's last scene,
    The end is neared;
At last I face death's somber screen,
The fleeting joys which intervene
    Have disappeared.

And as a panoramic scroll
    The past unreels;
The mocking past, beyond control,
Though buried, as a parchment roll,

Its tale reveals.

I stand before the dread, unknown,
    Yet solemn fact;
I see the seeds of folly sown
In wayward years, maturely grown,
    Nor can retract.

My weaknesses rise to my sight;
    And now, too late,
I fain would former actions right,
Which years have buried in their flight;
    Now sealed by fate.

My frailties and iniquities
    I plainly see;
Committed acts accusive rise,
Omitted duties criticise
    In mockery.

I feel I have offended oft,
    E'en at my best
Have failed to guide my course aloft;
Perhaps in trival hour, have scoffed
    With idle jest.

Prone to misgiving, prone to doubt,
    And frail from birth;
More light and frivolous than devout;
With life's brief candle flickering out,
    I speed from earth.

Can grief excuse indifference

With groan or tear?
Can deep remorse and penitence,
Or anguish mitigate offense
    With pang sincere?

Ah! Tears can ne'er unlock the past
    Which opens not;
And what is done is welded fast,
Through all eternity to last,
    Nor change one jot.

Whate'er may lie beyond the veil
    I calmly face,
And sink, as grievous tears bewail
My faults and imperfections frail,
    In death's embrace.

And as I think the matter o'er,
    Pensive and sad,
While its shortcomings I deplore,
The fruits which my existence bore
    Were not all bad.

From all which can rejoice or grieve
    I shortly go,
And now, in life's declining eve
I wonder, hope, try to believe--
    Soon I shall know!

My spirit flees, as night enwraps,
    To its reward;
The earth recedes, I feel it lapse;
I sink as dissolution snaps

The silver cord.

O, Thou whose presence I can feel
    Each hour I live,
While passing through death's stern ordeal,
Wilt Thou Thy mercy still reveal,
    And still forgive?

# Deprive This Strange and Complex World.

Deprive this strange and complex world
  Of all the charms of art;
Deprive it of those sweeter joys
  Which music doth impart;
But oh, preserve that smile, which tells
  The secret of the heart!

The world may lose its massive piles
  Which point their spires above;
May spare the tuneful nightingale
  And gently cooing dove;
But woe betide it, if it lose
  The sentiment of love!

# The Legend of St. Regimund.

St. Regimund, e'er he became a saint,
Was much imbued with vulgar earthly taint;
E'er he renounced the honors of a Knight
And doffed his coat of mail and helmet bright,
For sober cassock and monastic hood,
Leaving the castle for the cloister rude,
And changed the banquet's sumptuous repast
For frugal crusts and the ascetic fast;
Forsook his charger and equipments for
The crucifix and sacerdotal war;
While yet with valiant sword and blazoned shield
He braved the dangers of the martial field,
Or sought the antlered trophies of the chase
In forest and sequestered hunting place;
Or, tiring of the hunt's exciting sport,
Enjoyed the idle pleasures of the court,
Whiling away the time with games of chance,
With music and the more voluptuous dance,
The hollow paths of vanity pursued,
Laughed, jested, swore, drank, danced, and even wooed;
No tongue more prone to questionable wit,
Nor chaste, when time and place demanded it;
His basso voice, both voluble and strong,
Excelled in wassail mirth and ribald song;
He swore with oaths most impious and unblest;
Ate much, drank more, on these lines did his best;
Caroused by day, caroused by candle light,
In fact behaved like any other knight.

This medieval knight (the legend saith)
For months would scarcely draw a sober breath;
But as his appetite grew more and more
Drank each day worse than on the day before;
Was drunk all night, all day continued so,
Indulged in every vice he chanced to know.
But long debauch and riotous excess
Reduce their strongest votaries to distress;
When nature can the strain no longer stand
She chastens with a sure and irate hand,
So when the day of reckoning had come,
She smote with fever and delirium
This valiant knight whom we have tried to paint;
A very slim foundation for a saint!

The crisis reached, his fever stricken brain
Surrendered reason to excessive pain;
Nor moment's respite, comatose and kind,
Relieved the raging furnace of his mind;
And gruesome spectres, awful and unreal,
Through his disordered vagaries would steal;
When last his scorching temples sought repose
In hasty nap or intermittent doze,
His eyes beheld, though starting from his head,
A grizzly figure leaning o'er his bed,
With aspect foul beyond descriptive word,
As one for months in sepulchre interred,
Restored again to animated breath,
A weird composite type of life and death;
With countenance most hideous and vile,
Leering with ghastly and unearthly smile;
Pointing its shriveled finger, as in scorn,
Of mockery and accusation born.

As he beheld in terror and surprise
This gruesome shape which mocked before his eyes
He could distinguish in its haughty mien
A bearing, something as his own had been;
Nor had its withered visage quite the look
Of vampire, ghoul or evanescent spook;
And as the apparition o'er him bent,
He saw that every seam or lineament,
Contour of feature, prominence of bone,
Bore all a striking semblance to his own.

The horror stricken knight essayed to speak,
But words responded tremulous and weak,
And mustering his dissipated strength,
A sitting posture he assumed at length,--
"Whate'er thou art, thou harbinger of gloom,
Thou fiend or ghoul, fresh from the new made tomb,
Thou vampire, diabolical and fell,
Thou stygian shade or denizen of hell,
I charge thee, thing of evil, to confess
Why thou hast thus disturbed my sore distress.
Why hast thou burst my chamber's bolted door
Where guest unbidden never trod before?
Break this suspense, so horrible and still!
Declare thy tidings, be they good or ill,
Be thou from Heaven or from the realms below.
I charge thee speak, be thou a friend or foe;
Break thou thy silence, ominous and deep,
Or hence! Pursue thy way and let me sleep!"

The grizzly spectre, still more ghastly grown,
Surveyed with visage obdurate as stone,

Then smiled with grimace of derisive craft,
And in a most repugnant manner, laughed,
But all the knight discerned with eye and ear,
Was his own maudlin laugh and drunken leer.
"Breathe thou thy message," shrieked the frantic knight
"Discharge thy purpose, though it blast and blight,
I charge thee, speak, by all that is most fair.
By all most foul, I charge thee to declare;
By my bright armor and my trusty sword;
I charge thee, speak, by Holy Rood and Word!"
He sank exhausted, in such pallid fright
The snowy sheets looked dark beside such white.
The spectre paused in silence for awhile,
Then broke into a most repulsive smile,
And answered in a weird and hollow tone,
Enough to freeze the marrow in the bone:
"I am thy blasted spirit's counterpart,
A body fit for thy most evil heart,
I am thy life, its psychic image sent
To bear thee company, till thou repent."

'Tis said, for forty days the spectre stayed.
For forty days the knight incessant prayed;
With scourge, with vigil and ascetic rite,
With fast, with groan remorseful and contrite,
He cleansed his blackened spirit by degrees,
And purified it from its vanities;
And as he prayed, the spectre's gruesome scowl
Grew day by day less hideous and foul,
As he waxed holy, it became more bright;
And after forty days, arrayed in white
It spread its spotless arms, devoid of taint
Above this erstwhile knight and henceforth saint

In benediction, as he knelt in prayer,--
Then vanished instantly to empty air.

Such is the tale, embellished by the Muse,
'Tis true or false, believe it as you choose;
Some folks accept the story out and out,
While some prefer to entertain a doubt.
But if it be fictitious and unreal,
'Tis not subscribed and sworn, and bears no seal;
It points a moral, as the legend old,
If it conveys it, 'twas not vainly told,
For should I such an apparition see--
I think t'would almost make a monk of me.

# As The Indian.

Lo, the poor Indian, whose untutored mind
Sees God in the clouds and hears Him in the wind.
--Pope.

Within the wind, my untaught ear
  The voice of Deity can hear,
And in the fleeting cloud discern
  His movements, vast and taciturn;
    For in the universe I trace
    The wondrous grandeur of His face.

I see him in each blade of grass,
  Each towering peak and mountain pass;

Each forest, river, lake and fen
  Reveals the God of worlds and men;
    His works of wisdom prove to me,
    A wise, creative Deity.


# The Fragrant Perfume of the Flowers.


The fragrant perfume of the flowers,
Exuding in the summer hours,
E'en as the altar's incense rare
Disseminated through the air,
May never reach the azure skies,
Yet can the earth aromatize.

And so the voice of secret prayer,
Ascending on the wings of air,
Though it should reach no listening ear,
Of Deity inclined to hear,
Still soothes the anguish of the mind,
And leaves a tranquil peace behind.

# An Answer.

When passing years have streaked with frost
  These tresses now as jet,
When life's meridian is crossed
  And beauty's sun has set,
When youth's last fleeting charm is lost,
  Wilt thou be constant yet,
Nor time thy sentiment exhaust
  And cause thee to forget?
    If so--
     My answer, I confess,
  Shall be a calm, decided "Yes";
    But otherwise a "No"!

# Fame.

There is a cliff, no matter where,
  Which softened by the agencies
Of rain, exposure to the air,
  And alternating thaw and freeze,
    Most readily admits the edge
    Of chisel, or the sharpened wedge.

The travelers, while passing by,
  Within its shade find welcome rest;

And one of them mechanically,
　As is a custom in the west,
　　Upon its surface stern and gray
　　Carved out his name, and went his way.

Though inartistic and uncouth,
　That effort of a novice hand
Exemplifies a striking truth,
　And may Time's ravages withstand,
　　To be by future ages read,
　　When years and centuries have fled.

So on life's mighty thoroughfare,
　The multitude of every class
Leave no inscriptions chiseled, where
　Their transient footsteps chanced to pass,
And waft to each succeeding age
　No echoes from their pilgrimage.

Though many pass, yet few record
　Their names in characters sublime,
By grand achievement, work or word
　Upon the monolith of Time;
　　But few inscribe a lasting name
　　On the eternal cliffs of Fame.

# The First Storm.

The leafless branch and meadow sere,
   The dull and leaden skies,
Join with the mournful wind and drear
In dirges for the passing year,
   Which unreturning flies.

The night in starless gloom descends,
   Nor can the pale moonshine
Break through the clouds whose veil extends
In boundless form, and darkly blends
   With the horizon's line.

Fond nature, in a playful mood,
   In cover of the night,
Arrays the plain and forest rude,
The city and the solitude,
   In robe of spotless white.

# Thoughts.

I dug a grave, one smiling April day,
  A grave whose small proportions testified
To empty arms, and playthings put away,
  To ears which heard, when only fancy cried;

I wondered, as I shaped that little mound,
If in my home such grief should e'er be found.

I dug a grave, 'twas in the month of June;
  A grave for one who at his zenith died;
When, on that mound with floral tributes strewn,
  The tear-drops fell of one but late his bride,
    I wondered if upon my silent bier
    Should rest the moist impression of a tear.

I dug a grave by Autumn's sober light,
  A grave of full dimensions; 'twas for one
Whose hair had changed its raven hue to white,
  Whose course had finished with the setting sun;
    I wondered, as I toiled with pick and spade,
    Where, and by whom, would my last home be made.


# From A Saxon Legend.


Within a vale in distant Saxony,
  In time uncertain, though 'twas long ago.
There dwelt a woman, most unhappily,
  From borrowed trouble, and imagined woe.

Hers was a husband generous, and kind,
  Her children, three, were not of uncouth mold;
Hers was a thatch which mocked at rain and wind,
  Within her secret purse were coins of gold.

The drouth had ne'er descended on her field,
  Nor had distemper sore distressed her kine;
The vine had given its accustomed yield,
  So that her casks were filled with ruddy wine.

Her sheep and goats waxed fat, and ample fleece
  Rewarded every harvest of the shear;
Her lambs all bleated in sequestered peace,
  Nor prowling wolf occasioned nightly fear.

With all she fretted, pined, and brooded sore,
  Harbored each slight vexation, courted grief,
Shut out the smiling sunshine from her door,
  And magnified each care to bas relief.

Still waxed her grievous burden more and more,
  Till, with a resolution, rash and blind,
At dead of night she fled her humble door,
  As if to leave her grievous load behind.

She journeyed as the night wore slowly on,
  Unmindful of the tuneful nightingale,
Till in due time her footsteps fell upon
  A hill, the demarcation of the vale.

As Lot's wife, in her flight, could not refrain
  From viewing foul Gomorrah's funeral pyre,
From one last glance across that ancient plain,
  At guilty Sodom wreathed in vengeful fire;

So when this woman reached the summit's crest,
  She turned her eyes in one last farewell look,
The fruitful vale lay stretched in placid rest,

And all was silent save the breeze and brook.

The moon in partial fullness, mild, serene,
  Flooding the landscape with her mellow light,
Illumined every old familiar scene,
  Brought their associations to her sight.

When, lo! as if by touch of magic wand,
  On every roof, of tile, of thatch or wood,
As instantly as magic doth respond,
  A cross, of various size and form there stood.

O'er homes unknown to frown or grievous word,
  O'er homes where laughter hid the silent wail,
O'er homes where discontent was never heard,
  Huge crosses glistened in the moonlight pale.

A cross o'er every habitation rose,
  O'er ducal palace, and the cottage small
Where slept the husbandman in deep repose;
  And, lo, her cross was smallest of them all!

# Christmas Chimes.

Once more the merry Christmas bells,
  Are ringing far and wide;
Their chime in rhythmic chorus swells,
  While every brazen throat foretells,
  A joyous Christmastide.

What is the burden of your chime,
　Ye bells of Christmastide?
What tidings in your clangorous rhyme,
What message would your tongues sublime
　To human hearts confide?

　Our chime is of salvation's plan,
　　And every Christmastide
Since Christmas bells to chime, began
　We've caroled Heaven's gift to man,
　　A Saviour crucified.

# The Unknowable.

O! Sun, resplendent in the smiling morn,
　As thou dost view the wastes of earth and sky,
Canst thou behold the realms of the Unborn,
　Canst thou behold the realms of those who die?
Where dwells the spirit e'er its mortal birth,
　　E'er yet it suffereth
The pain and sorrow incident to earth?
　　Where after death?
The Sun gave answer, with refulgent glow:
Child of a fleeting hour, thou too must die to know.

Canst tell, thou jeweled canopy of space,
　Bewildering, and boundless to the eyes,
Knowest thou the unborn spirits' dwelling place?
　Knowest thou the distant regions of the skies

Where rest the spirits freed from mundane strife,
    From mortal grief and care?
Knowest thou the secret of the future life?
    Canst thou tell where?
From Space infinite echoed the reply:
Child of a transient day, thou too, to know, must die.

Ye Winds who blow and cleave the formless skies,
  Ye Winds who blow with desolating breath,
Can ye reveal pre-natal mysteries,
  And can ye solve the mystery of death?
Within thy ambient and viewless folds
    Imprisoned in the air,
May not the spirits wait their earthly moulds?
    Then tell ye where.
The answer came invisible and low:
Frail child of earthly clay, thou too must die to know.

What are your tidings, O ye raging Seas?
  Do your waves wash the islands of the blest,
Or view the Gardens of Hesperides?
  Know you the unborn spirits' place of rest?
And do your waters lave that unknown shore?
    And when the night is gone,
Shall the freed spirit, tired and faint no more,
    Behold the dawn?
The sad sea murmured, as its waves rolled high:
As all those gone before, thou, too, to know, must die.

# The Suicide.

What anguish rankled 'neath that silent breast?
 What spectral figures mocked those staring eyes,
 Luring them on to Stygian mysteries?
What overpowering sense of grief distressed?

What desperation nerved that rigid hand
 To pull the trigger with such deadly aim?
 What deep remorse, or terror, overcame
The dread inherent, of death's shadowy strand?

Perhaps the hand of unrelenting fate
 Fell with such tragic pressure, that the mind
 In frenzy, uncontrollable and blind,
Sought but the darkness, black and desolate.

Perhaps 'twas some misfortune's stunning blight,
 Perhaps unmerited, though deep disgrace,
 Or vision of a wronged accusing face
Pictured indelibly before the sight.

Perhaps the gnawing of some secret sin,
 Some aberration fraught with morbid gloom,
 A buried hope which ever burst its tomb,
Despondency, disaster, or chagrin.

That heart which throbbed in pain and discontent
 Is silent as the grave for which it yearned;
 That brain, which once with proud ambition burned,
Now oozes through the bullet's ghastly rent.

Those eyes, transfixed with such a gruesome stare,
  Once beamed with laughter, innocent and bright;
  The morning gave no presage of the night;
A smile may be the prelude of despair.

Whate'er his secret, it remains untold,
  For why to human anguish add one groan?
  Is grief the deeper grief because unknown?
So let the grave his form and burden hold.

Ye who have felt no crushing weight of care,
  From blame profuse, in charity refrain;
  Some depths of sorrow overwhelm the brain,
Some loads too great for human strength to bear.

# I Think When I Stand in the Presence of Death.

I think when I stand in the presence of Death,
  How futile is earthy endeavor,
If it be, with the flight of the last labored breath,
  The tongue has been silenced forever.

For no message is flashed from the lustreless eyes,
  When clos-ed so languid and weary,
And no voice from the darkness re-echoes our cries,
  In response to the agonized query!

We gaze at the solemn mysterious shroud
  With a vague and insatiate yearning,

And perceive but the sombre exterior cloud,
  With our vision of no discerning.

Not a whispering sound, not a glimmer of light,
  From that shadowy strand uncertain;
But He who ordained the day and night,
  Framed also Death's silent curtain.

# Hope.

Hope is the shadowy essence of a wish,
  A fond desire which floats before our eyes;
With lurid aberration, feverish,--
  We clutch the shadow which elusive, flies;
Though at our grasp the mocking fancy flees,
Hope still pursues and soothes realities.

Hope, as a mirage on the desert waste,
  Lures the lost traveler, by a vision fair
Of gushing fountains which he may not taste,
  Of streamlets cool depicted on the air;
With tongue outstretched and parched he onward speeds,
But as he moves the phantom scene recedes.

In the foul dungeon or the narrow cell,
  The prisoner doth pace his lonely beat,
And as he treads, his shackles clank a knell
  Responsive to each movement of his feet;
Yet through his grated window, he discerns

The star of hope which ever brightly burns.

A noble ship her ponderous anchor weighs,
  Glides from the harbor and is lost to sight;
A young wife waves farewell. As many days
  In passing turn her golden tresses white,
She scans the horizon through a mist of tears,
Hopes for that vanished sail which ne'er appears.

A galley slave in age and clime remote,
  Chained to his seat, unwilling plies the oar;
Before his eyes fond dreams of freedom float,
  He hopes amid the battle's crash and roar;
And as the waves the imprisoned wretches drown,
Hopes, as his fetters draw him swiftly down.

A mighty host in force of arms we see,
  With march invasive, cross a boundary line;
At its approach no freemen turn and flee,
  Each with his life defends his family shrine;
As burning homes illuminate the sky
With ghastly light, they hope and fight and die.

Beside the bed where rests the pallid form,
  Of loved one stricken with the fever's breath,
E'en when the loving hands, no longer warm,
  Portend the sure and swift approach of Death,
Hope holds the spirit in its house of clay,
And with that spirit only, soars away.

The guilty wretch, for murder doomed to die,
  Hoped, in his dungeon as the death watch paced,
Hoped, as the death cap veiled his evil eye,

Hoped, as the noose around his neck was placed,
Hoped, as the chaplain read his final prayer,
Hoped, as he struggled in the viewless air.

In the glad sunshine of life's vernal spring,
　Hope buoys the spirit with expectancy;
Hope with her dulcet voice and fluttering wing,
　Sings of life's goal with siren harmony;
When silvered temples tell that life declines,
That goal, though yet unreached, still brightly shines.

Yes! As through failure and vicissitude,
　We sail along with many an adverse wind,
Hope plants her beacon in the tempest rude,
　And leads with generous radiance unconfined;
And when the yawning grave receives its prey,
Hope speeds the spirit on its astral way.

## Metabole.

## AN APOSTROPHE TO THE MOON.

O, silvery moon, fair mistress of the night,
Thou mellow, ever vaccilating orb,
How many eons of unmeasured time
Hast thou, observant from thy astral poise,
Thy ever-changing station in the skies,
Beheld the wastes of earth, of air and space--
Ruling the waters, and the sombre night?

Pale queen of night, fair coquette of the skies,
Thou, who with fickle, sweet inconstancy
Receives the smile from the admiring sun,
And straight transmits it to the sordid earth,--
How many cycles of the silent past
Hast thou beheld the rise and fall of man,
His proud ascendency and swift decline;
His zenith and his pitiful decay;
E'er he emerged from out the dismal cave,
His habitation rude and primitive;
E'er yet the forest trembled at his stroke,
E'er his indenting chisel cleaved the stones

And framed the first crude human domicile?

As time rolled on and human skill advanced
By almost imperceptible degrees
Of slow, experimental tutorage,
Along a nobler, more artistic plane,
He hewed the stones in form of ornament,
Sculptured device of various design,
Embellishment of cunning symmetry,
Man's first attempt to scale the realms of art.

Thou hast beheld him on his suppliant kneel,
Engaged in worship, audible or mute,
Invoking thy protection and thy aid,
Thy gracious favor and beatitude;
With arms outstretched in reverential awe,
Propitiating thee, with fervent prayer
For the remission of thy baleful stroke.
Thou hast beheld his superstitious fear
And heard his curses, and his solemn prayers
As thy dark form eclipsed the smiling sun.

Thou hast beheld him fashion and adorn
The gorgeous altar and the totem pole;
With fervent zeal, and blind simplicity,
From base materials of wood or stone,
Carve out a God, then kneel and worship it.

Thou, too, hast heard the slave-whip's poignant crack,
The sound of avarice and turpitude,
As hands unwilling plied their arduous task,
Creating monuments to iron will,
Human injustice, greed and servitude.

Thou hast beheld him shape the pyramids,
Heap up the mound and build the massive wall,
Create the castle and the towering spire,
The ponderous dome and stately edifice.

*    *    *    *    *

From thy observant orbit in the skies,
Did'st thou behold that sacrilegious tower,
Which reared its massive form on Babel's plain,
Built by misguided and presumptuous men,
In vain and ineffectual attempt
To scale the heavens surreptitiously?

E'er the completion of the impious pile,
Thou mayest have heard, with silent nonchalance,
That strange catastrophe of human speech,
That dire confusion of the languages,
Confounding all the tongues and dialects
To unknown chaos of peculiar sounds.

Changing the conversation of the day
To accents strange and unintelligible,
Unlike to common and accepted terms;
To tones mysterious and unnatural,
Conglomerated forms of utterance
Which bore no semblance to the human voice.
Some rent the air with unaccustomed words
Striving in desperation to converse,
With ears which heard, but could not understand.

Some cursed, with oaths unknown to all but them,
While some essayed to frame the words of prayer,

Or to articulate the stern command,
And one, in most supreme authority,
Declaimed a ponderous regal ordinance,
But heard a sea of unfamiliar sounds,
Confused and desultory turbulence, and dissonance of harsh,
     discordant tones,
Instead of due attention and applause;
Nor were his words and usual forms of speech
Respected by the idle, wondering craft,
Which lately comprehended and obeyed.

Workmen addressed each other, but conveyed
No sense of meaning in their jargonings;
Nor had cognizance from the stammered tones,
Answered in turn, in verbal nothingness;
The crabbed cynic might no longer rail;
Nor those of sober countenance discourse
In melancholy and foreboding strains;
Nor light and frivolous sons of levity
On others perpetrate the humorous jest;
Fathers attempted to correct their sons,
Who, listening with filial reverence,
Heard but unknown and strange garrulity.

Some shrank in terror, as their ears discerned
Their own distorted efforts to converse;
Some ran in aimless frenzy to and fro,
Falling upon the earth with frantic cries;
Some stood in gaping wonder, nor perceived
The dire calamity, which bound them all
In one unbroken chain of misery.
Some beat their breasts in paroxysmal woe;
Some wore the driveling look of idiocy;

Some lost their reason and serenely smiled;
Some stalked with features imperturbable,
Finding no tear nor vent for their distress;
Some groaned, some shrieked, some wept in their despair,
Relaxing all attempts at vocal speech;
Some recognized the face but not the voice
Of some familiar friend, and grasped the hand,
Spoke with the eyes, when words no longer served.

\*     \*     \*     \*     \*

Did'st thou behold that temple which arose
On Mount Moriah's slope, the proud result
Of the endeavors of a noble race,
Whose tireless energy and wondrous skill
In architecture and the various arts
Were famed throughout the world; whose nimble hands
Carved out the pillar and the pedestal,
The column, polished and cylindrical,
The slab and ornamented architrave
From Parian marble of unblemished hue;
With stately cedars from the sloping sides
Of proud but long denuded Lebanon,
Erected that superb and marvelous pile
Whose wondrous grandeur and imposing form,
Correct proportions and true symmetry
And perfect uniformity of shape,
Beauty of contour and embellishment,
Splendor of finish and magnificence,
Excelled the proudest edifice of earth--
A fitting tribute to the Deity?

\*     \*     \*     \*     \*

Thou hast beheld the triumphs of his skill
Touched by the desolating hand of time,
Crumble, disintegrate and pass away--
Resolved to pristine particles of dust.

His strongest castle, bold and insolent,
Of warlike aspect and defiant mien,
With wall and rampart unassailable,
Impregnable to the assaults of man--
Surrender at the mold's insidious tread.

    Thou hast beheld
His palace and his most exalted courts
Bestrewn with fragments of the Peristyle;
The broken column, slab and monolith
O'erhung with pendant moss and slimy mold;
Its dismal haunts and gloomy apertures
Become the habitation of the bat,
The hissing serpent and the scorpion,
The basking lizard dull and indolent,
And forms of reptile, foul and venomous.

The throne where ruled the king with iron sway
Is vacant as the empty wastes of air,
Is ruled by desolation and decay.
No more the sceptered voice in stern command
Rings through its halls, nor can the dazzling flash
Of the tiara and the diadem,
The ensign and insignia of power,
The emblazoned crest and jeweled coat of arms,

Or proud escutcheon of illustrious name
Excite with envy or inspire with fear.

The boisterous carousal and the sound
Of wassail mirth, inebriate and loud,
And midnight revelry, is hushed and still.

      Time shifts the scenes--
The haughty prince and the most abject slave,
Who cowered and trembled 'neath his austere glance,
The fawning and ignoble sycophant,
The courtier and the basest serf, have met
On equal terms beneath the silent dust.

From thy celestial 'minions thou hast seen
His proudest temples sink into decay,
Grim desolation and desuetude;
The silent hush succeed the plaintive hymn,
The anthem cease to swell in rhythmic praise,
Or vaulted dome re-echo with the sound
Of pipe, of organ, harp and dulcimer;
The voice of sacerdotal eloquence
Become as silent as the unborn thought;
The fragrant perfume of the frankincense,
The scent of swinging censor and of myrrh,
Supplanted by foul odors of decay;
The sacred flame extinguished and forgot,
Its votaries and congregations fled;
The forms who ministered and forms who knelt,
The burnished altar and the hoary priest,
Commingling their atoms in the dust.

\*   \*   \*   \*   \*

Thou, too, hast heard the clash of hostile arms,
The blast of trumpet and the martial tread,
The neigh of charger anxious for the fray,
The din and the confusion of the fight,
The noise and turmoil of contending hosts,
The crunch of breaking bones and shrieks of pain;
The angry challenge and defiant taunt,
The cries of rage and curses of despair,
The dying groan and gnash of clench-ed teeth,
The plea for mercy, with uplifted arms,
As through the bosom plunged the ruthless steel;
The clank of shackles and the captives groan,
As marched the vanquished forth to servitude,
To ceaseless toil rewarded by the scourge;
To stand within the slave marts and endure
The taunts and bear the chains of slavery.

Did'st thou look down with neutral radiance
On that incursion from the Scythian plain,
A surging multitude beyond the power
Of mental computation and which seemed
A seething mass of spears and shapes of war,
A sea of bellicose barbarity,
O'erwhelming helpless and ill-fated Tyre
With a resistless deluge of the sword?

Or when that vast and uncomputed horde
Swept westward from the steppes of Tartary
With stern Atilla riding at its head,
Leaving in ruthless Mongol truculence,

Awake, both red and blackened by the torch;
The scourge[6], perhaps of God, perhaps of Hell!

Did'st thou not flinch when t'ward the Christian west
The fell invasion of the Saracen
Headed its course with crimson scimitar;
Supplanting the mild precepts of the Cross
With those of lust, of hate and bigotry?

&ast;　　&ast;　　&ast;　　&ast;　　&ast;

Did'st thou not weep when proud Atlantis sunk
Beneath the surging and engulfing waves,
The aftermath of Earth's most tragic shock;
Or when the ark, upon that greatest flood,
Which from the black and pregnant heavens fell.
For forty days and forty weary nights,
Above the ruins of a deluged world,
Floated in safety with its living freight?

Did'st Thou look down in idle apathy,
When grim Vesuvius, from his dormant rest
Awoke, in molten fury, and o'ercame
With liquid flood and scoriaceous hail
The sleeping cities which beneath him lay;
Interring with such fiery burial
That neither remnant nor inhabitant
Escaped from that both grave and funeral pyre;
Nor vestige of their proud magnificence
Rose from the scene with charred and blackened form;

---

6    Atilla was believed by the early Christians to have been a scourge sent direct from God, and some historians aver that he himself encouraged the belief.

And rolling centuries, in passing, left
But dim remembrance in the minds of men?

Did'st thou, in age more ancient and remote,
Gaze from thy poise with cold complacency
Upon the guilty cities[7] of the plain,
Surcharged with lust and the extremes of sin,
Which Holy Writ avers, when 'neath the shower
Of well deserved combustion from the skies,
They sunk in conflagration with their vice;
And perishing, to ages yet to come
Bequeathed a foul and blasted heritage,
An infamous and execrated name?

\* \* \* \* \*

Art thou to human anguish so inured
That thou hast neither sentiment of grief
Nor sense of pity for terrestrial ills?
Can agonizing and heart-rending scenes
Relax thy obdurate and placid face
To semblance of emotion? Can man's woes
Excite thy tranquil immobility
To the pathetic look of tenderness,
Or touch thy bosom's calm indifference
With profuse throbs of sympathetic ruth?
Can'st thou unmoved behold the widow's tears,
Or those of orphaned childish innocence,
Or those which wondering infant eyes have shed
On unresponsive breasts, which nevermore
Throb with maternal warmth and suckle them?
Can'st thou with cold, unsympathizing light

---

7   Sodom and Gommorah.

Illuminate the ruined maid's despair
Without the echo of a lunar groan?
Hast thou no pang of sorrow or regret
For guilty man, nor tear for his distress,
Or are the tides within thy moist control
The copious weepings of thy mellow lids--
Thy sea of teardrops shed for human woes?

*     *     *     *     *

Did'st thou behold, when that most favored star,
Transcending in refulgence all the orbs
Of boundless and bejewelled firmament,
With flash of overwhelming brilliancy
Plunged through the wondering heavens, whose pale spheres
In contrast dimmed to insignificance,
And gliding through the twinkling realms of space,
Burst with such splendor as the envious stars
Had never witnessed since the heavens stood;
Halting in glory o'er Judea's plain?

Halted and burned in stellar reverence,
Above a fold where wrapped in swaddling clothes
A new-born infant in a manger lay;
In humble contrast to the throne of light,
He left to tread the thorny paths of earth;
In undefiled and stainless innocence,
Which earth with all her foul iniquities
Might never tarnish nor pollute with sin.

Perhaps upon that sage triumvirate
Which journeyed from the famed and affluent East,
In regal pomp and rich munificence,

To lay their costly presents at His feet
And worship at that new-born infant's shrine,
Thou shed'st thy mellow rays and lit the way
O'er deserts to the hills of Bethlehem;
Dividing honors with that prince of stars.

Wert thou a witness on that selfsame night
When humble shepherds on Judea's hills,
Watching their flocks with all attentive care,
Beheld unwonted grandeur in the skies?
The ordinary stars were glittering
In unaccustomed glory, and the orbs
Which twinkle in that pale celestial train
Which cleaves in twain the ambient universe,
Had changed their milky hue to that of gold;
But all the forms of stellar brilliancy
Made way for that most bright and luminous
Which glowed with holy radiance, which might
Not emanate from aught but sacred star;
Dispensing such serene magnificence
That e'en the admiring heavens stood abashed.

      At such a sight,
Though savoring more of blessing than of curse,
Small marvel 'twas their unenlightened minds
Were seized with sudden and peculiar fear,
So that their trembling knees together smote.
And as they stood
In awestruck trepidation and alarm
The heavens as the bifurcated door
Of some familiar, hospitable tent,
Parted their gorgeous curtains and disclosed
A multitude of the celestial host,

Numerous beyond all efforts to compute,
Solemn of countenance, yet beautiful
Beyond the comprehension of the eye,
Surging in such immaculate array
Of various raiment as the stainless white
Of snows which countless centuries have placed
On rugged Ararat's tremendous heights,
Were blended in an essence!

      Then for a moment's time
The heavens were silent as those forms were fair;
Then instantly throughout the realms of light
Was heard a crash in sacred unison,
As all the trumpets and the harps of heaven
And all the varied instruments of earth
Had burst in one grand, detonating chord;
Now rose the quavering, vibratory tones
Of flageolet and solitary reed;
Now as a blending of all instruments
In echoing harmonics, sweet and low,
In soft reverberating resonance;
The voice of cornet and sonorous horn
Blent with the warbling accents of the flute
And chime of mellow bells, unknown to earth;
Paean of dulcimer and harpsichord
In combination of concordant tone,
Melting the stars with dulcet symphony.

But sweeter than those instruments of joy,
Tuned by angelic fingers, rose the strains
Of vocal concord and mellifluence,
As swelled in chorus those seraphic throats
In falling cadence and ecstatic flight,

Surpassing heaven's grandest melody
In all that appertains to choral song!
The acme of celestial harmony
Which angel ears discerned with glad surprise;
But sweeter than that song, the glad refrain
Wafted from angel tongues innumerable,
To earth and the inhabitants thereof,
"Peace! Peace on Earth, the Deity's Good Will!"

         *       *       *       *       *

Didst thou not shrink, when on Golgotha's crest
Three crosses as three grizzly spectres rose,
Spreading their ghastly arms protestingly,
In silent malediction o'er the scene,
And even nature paused and stood aghast
In shuddering horror at the awful sight,
Relaxing with the trembling earthquake shock
Her sympathetic tension?
And when the lightning rent the canopy
Of black sepulchral clouds, which like a shroud
Enveloped earth on that terrific night,
They lit a face compassionate and pure,
E'en from beneath the cruel crown of thorns
Glancing in pity, kindled not with wrath
At his tormentors, those who loved him not--
The multitude which surged about the cross
Cursing with accents vile and crying loud,
Crucify Him! Crucify Him!

"Rejected and despised of men--"
Earth, which hath ever slain her noblest sons,
Slays also her Redeemer!

\*     \*     \*     \*     \*

Creation is but systematized decay,
And ***Change*** is blazoned on the very skies,
As in ephemeral telluric scenes,
And through the whole cosmogony of worlds,
Is written and rewritten!

Thou who hast seen the stately mastodon
Roam at his will o'er earth's prolific plains,
And the unwieldy megatherium
Dragging his cumbrous, disproportioned weight
Through quaternary marsh and stagnant fen;
Or watched the ichthyosaurus plow the seas,
Churning the waters till the glistening foam
Rode on the greenish undulating waves;
And huge saurian and reptilian shapes
Amphibious and pelagic, swim and crawl,
Cleaving the waters with tremendous strokes,
Writhing with foul contortions in disport,
Splashing and laving in the thermal seas
Of the remote and prehistoric past;
Thou who hast seen them fail and pass away
Shalt also shine when man has disappeared.

Thou who hast seen the rank luxuriance
Of vegetation flourish and decay,
Vanish and pass away insensibly,
Perish from off the earth which nourished it,
And time supplant its rich exuberance
With arid wastes of bleak sterility;
Wilt thou look down in silent unconcern

When countless eons of denuding time
Have rendered earth as barren as thyself,
Bereft of verdure's last habiliment;
When men, with all their passions and desires,
Their strange combines of evil and of good,
Their proud achievements and exalted aims
Have passed away forever?

The universe is but a sepulcher
For worlds defunct, as earth for living forms!
And thou, O Moon, who hast surveyed all this
Thyself shalt be consumed with fervent heat,
For e'en the firmament shall pass away.

\*    \*    \*    \*    \*

Supreme Intelligence,
Thou who createst worlds and satellites,
(And Who canst estimate the universe)
Weighing the heavens in Thy balances,
Who hast ordained the laws of cosmic space
To guide aright the planetary spheres;
Thou Ruler of the infinite and great,
Alike of vast and infinitesimal;
Thou fundamental cause of all that is,
In process of creation and decay,
In the mutation and the ravages
Sequent of constant lapse and flight of time
Reveal Thy laws that we may follow them:
Help us to recognize in all Thy works,
Whether of atom or stupendous mass,
The hand of Deity.

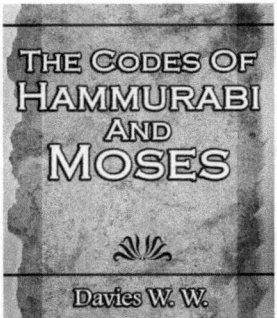

### The Codes Of Hammurabi And Moses
### W. W. Davies

QTY

The discovery of the Hammurabi Code is one of the greatest achievements of archaeology, and is of paramount interest, not only to the student of the Bible, but also to all those interested in ancient history...

**Religion**    **ISBN:** *1-59462-338-4*    **Pages:132**
*MSRP $12.95*

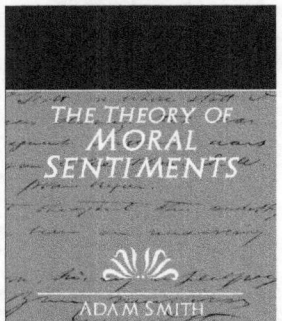

### The Theory of Moral Sentiments
### Adam Smith

QTY

This work from 1749. contains original theories of conscience amd moral judgment and it is the foundation for systemof morals.

**Philosophy**  **ISBN:** *1-59462-777-0*    **Pages:536**
*MSRP $19.95*

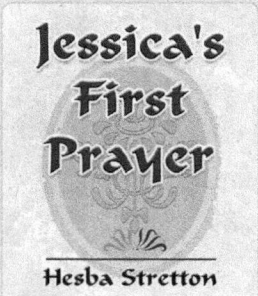

### Jessica's First Prayer
### Hesba Stretton

QTY

In a screened and secluded corner of one of the many railway-bridges which span the streets of London there could be seen a few years ago, from five o'clock every morning until half past eight, a tidily set-out coffee-stall, consisting of a trestle and board, upon which stood two large tin cans, with a small fire of charcoal burning under each so as to keep the coffee boiling during the early hours of the morning when the work-people were thronging into the city on their way to their daily toil...

**Childrens**    **ISBN:** *1-59462-373-2*    **Pages:84**
*MSRP $9.95*

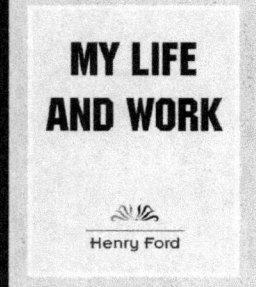

### My Life and Work
### Henry Ford

QTY

Henry Ford revolutionized the world with his implementation of mass production for the Model T automobile. Gain valuable business insight into his life and work with his own auto-biography... "We have only started on our development of our country we have not as yet, with all our talk of wonderful progress, done more than scratch the surface. The progress has been wonderful enough but..."

**Biographies/**    **ISBN:** *1-59462-198-5*    **Pages:300**
*MSRP $21.95*

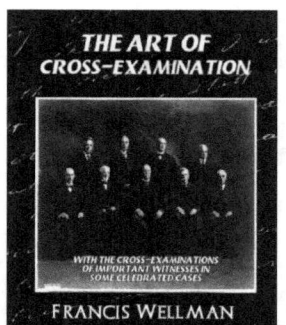

## The Art of Cross-Examination
## Francis Wellman

QTY

I presume it is the experience of every author, after his first book is published upon an important subject, to be almost overwhelmed with a wealth of ideas and illustrations which could readily have been included in his book, and which to his own mind, at least, seem to make a second edition inevitable. Such certainly was the case with me; and when the first edition had reached its sixth impression in five months, I rejoiced to learn that it seemed to my publishers that the book had met with a sufficiently favorable reception to justify a second and considerably enlarged edition. ..

**Reference**    **ISBN:** *1-59462-647-2*

**Pages:412**

*MSRP $19.95*

## On the Duty of Civil Disobedience
## Henry David Thoreau

QTY

Thoreau wrote his famous essay On the Duty of Civil Disobedience, as a protest against an unjust but popular war and the immoral but popular institution of slave-owning. He did more than write—he declined to pay his taxes, and was hauled off to gaol in consequence. Who can say how much this refusal of his hastened the end of the war and of slavery ?

**Law**    **ISBN:** *1-59462-747-9*

**Pages:48**

*MSRP $7.45*

## Dream Psychology Psychoanalysis for Beginners
## Sigmund Freud

QTY

Sigmund Freud, born Sigismund Schlomo Freud (May 6, 1856 - September 23, 1939), was a Jewish-Austrian neurologist and psychiatrist who co-founded the psychoanalytic school of psychology. Freud is best known for his theories of the unconscious mind, especially involving the mechanism of repression; his redefinition of sexual desire as mobile and directed towards a wide variety of objects; and his therapeutic techniques, especially his understanding of transference in the therapeutic relationship and the presumed value of dreams as sources of insight into unconscious desires.

**Psychology**    **ISBN:** *1-59462-905-6*

**Pages:196**

*MSRP $15.45*

## The Miracle of Right Thought
## Orison Swett Marden

QTY

Believe with all of your heart that you will do what you were made to do. When the mind has once formed the habit of holding cheerful, happy, prosperous pictures, it will not be easy to form the opposite habit. It does not matter how improbable or how far away this realization may see, or how dark the prospects may be, if we visualize them as best we can, as vividly as possible, hold tenaciously to them and vigorously struggle to attain them, they will gradually become actualized, realized in the life. But a desire, a longing without endeavor, a yearning abandoned or held indifferently will vanish without realization.

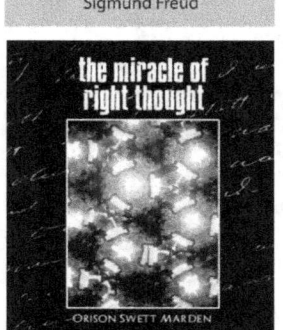

**Self Help**    **ISBN:** *1-59462-644-8*

**Pages:360**

*MSRP $25.45*

QTY

**The Rosicrucian Cosmo-Conception Mystic Christianity** *by Max Heindel*      ISBN: *1-59462-188-8*   **$38.95**
*The Rosicrucian Cosmo-conception is not dogmatic, neither does it appeal to any other authority than the reason of the student. It is: not controversial, but is: sent forth in the, hope that it may help to clear...*      New Age/Religion Pages 646

**Abandonment To Divine Providence** *by Jean-Pierre de Caussade*      ISBN: *1-59462-228-0*   **$25.95**
*"The Rev. Jean Pierre de Caussade was one of the most remarkable spiritual writers of the Society of Jesus in France in the 18th Century. His death took place at Toulouse in 1751. His works have gone through many editions and have been republished...*      Inspirational/Religion Pages 400

**Mental Chemistry** *by Charles Haanel*      ISBN: *1-59462-192-6*   **$23.95**
*Mental Chemistry allows the change of material conditions by combining and appropriately utilizing the power of the mind. Much like applied chemistry creates something new and unique out of careful combinations of chemicals the mastery of mental chemistry...*      New Age Pages 354

**The Letters of Robert Browning and Elizabeth Barret Barrett 1845-1846 vol II**      ISBN: *1-59462-193-4*   **$35.95**
*by Robert Browning and Elizabeth Barrett*      Biographies Pages 596

**Gleanings In Genesis (volume I)** *by Arthur W. Pink*      ISBN: *1-59462-130-6*   **$27.45**
*Appropriately has Genesis been termed "the seed plot of the Bible" for in it we have, in germ form, almost all of the great doctrines which are afterwards fully developed in the books of Scripture which follow...*      Religion/Inspirational Pages 420

**The Master Key** *by L. W. de Laurence*      ISBN: *1-59462-001-6*   **$30.95**
*In no branch of human knowledge has there been a more lively increase of the spirit of research during the past few years than in the study of Psychology, Concentration and Mental Discipline. The requests for authentic lessons in Thought Control, Mental Discipline and...*      New Age/Business Pages 422

**The Lesser Key Of Solomon Goetia** *by L. W. de Laurence*      ISBN: *1-59462-092-X*   **$9.95**
*This translation of the first book of the "Lernegton" which is now for the first time made accessible to students of Talismanic Magic was done, after careful collation and edition, from numerous Ancient Manuscripts in Hebrew, Latin, and French...*      New Age/Occult Pages 92

**Rubaiyat Of Omar Khayyam** *by Edward Fitzgerald*      ISBN:*1-59462-332-5*   **$13.95**
*Edward Fitzgerald, whom the world has already learned, in spite of his own efforts to remain within the shadow of anonymity, to look upon as one of the rarest poets of the century, was born at Bredfield, in Suffolk, on the 31st of March, 1809. He was the third son of John Purcell...*      Music Pages 172

**Ancient Law** *by Henry Maine*      ISBN: *1-59462-128-4*   **$29.95**
*The chief object of the following pages is to indicate some of the earliest ideas of mankind, as they are reflected in Ancient Law, and to point out the relation of those ideas to modern thought.*      Religion/History Pages 452

**Far-Away Stories** *by William J. Locke*      ISBN: *1-59462-129-2*   **$19.45**
*"Good wine needs no bush, but a collection of mixed vintages does. And this book is just such a collection. Some of the stories I do not want to remain buried for ever in the musty files of dead magazine-numbers an author's not unpardonable vanity..."*      Fiction Pages 272

**Life of David Crockett** *by David Crockett*      ISBN: *1-59462-250-7*   **$27.45**
*"Colonel David Crockett was one of the most remarkable men of the times in which he lived. Born in humble life, but gifted with a strong will, an indomitable courage, and unremitting perseverance...*      Biographies/New Age Pages 424

**Lip-Reading** *by Edward Nitchie*      ISBN: *1-59462-206-X*   **$25.95**
*Edward B. Nitchie, founder of the New York School for the Hard of Hearing, now the Nitchie School of Lip-Reading, Inc, wrote "LIP-READING Principles and Practice". The development and perfecting of this meritorious work on lip-reading was an undertaking...*      How-to Pages 400

**A Handbook of Suggestive Therapeutics, Applied Hypnotism, Psychic Science**      ISBN: *1-59462-214-0*   **$24.95**
*by Henry Munro*      Health/New Age/Health/Self-help Pages 376

**A Doll's House: and Two Other Plays** *by Henrik Ibsen*      ISBN: *1-59462-112-8*   **$19.95**
*Henrik Ibsen created this classic when in revolutionary 1848 Rome. Introducing some striking concepts in playwriting for the realist genre, this play has been studied the world over.*      Fiction/Classics/Plays 308

**The Light of Asia** *by sir Edwin Arnold*      ISBN: *1-59462-204-3*   **$13.95**
*In this poetic masterpiece, Edwin Arnold describes the life and teachings of Buddha. The man who was to become known as Buddha to the world was born as Prince Gautama of India but he rejected the worldly riches and abandoned the reigns of power when...*  Religion/History/Biographies Pages 170

**The Complete Works of Guy de Maupassant** *by Guy de Maupassant*      ISBN: *1-59462-157-8*   **$16.95**
*"For days and days, nights and nights, I had dreamed of that first kiss which was to consecrate our engagement, and I knew not on what spot I should put my lips..."*      Fiction/Classics Pages 240

**The Art of Cross-Examination** *by Francis L. Wellman*      ISBN: *1-59462-309-0*   **$26.95**
*Written by a renowned trial lawyer, Wellman imparts his experience and uses case studies to explain how to use psychology to extract desired information through questioning.*      How-to/Science/Reference Pages 408

**Answered or Unanswered?** *by Louisa Vaughan*      ISBN: *1-59462-248-5*   **$10.95**
*Miracles of Faith in China*      Religion Pages 112

**The Edinburgh Lectures on Mental Science (1909)** *by Thomas*      ISBN: *1-59462-008-3*   **$11.95**
*This book contains the substance of a course of lectures recently given by the writer in the Queen Street Hall, Edinburgh. Its purpose is to indicate the Natural Principles governing the relation between Mental Action and Material Conditions...*      New Age/Psychology Pages 148

**Ayesha** *by H. Rider Haggard*      ISBN: *1-59462-301-5*   **$24.95**
*Verily and indeed it is the unexpected that happens! Probably if there was one person upon the earth from whom the Editor of this, and of a certain previous history, did not expect to hear again...*      Classics Pages 380

**Ayala's Angel** *by Anthony Trollope*      ISBN: *1-59462-352-X*   **$29.95**
*The two girls were both pretty, but Lucy who was twenty-one who supposed to be simple and comparatively unattractive, whereas Ayala was credited, as her Bombwhat romantic name might show, with poetic charm and a taste for romance. Ayala when her father died was nineteen...*      Fiction Pages 484

**The American Commonwealth** *by James Bryce*      ISBN: *1-59462-286-8*   **$34.45**
*An interpretation of American democratic political theory. It examines political mechanics and society from the perspective of Scotsman James Bryce*      Politics Pages 572

**Stories of the Pilgrims** *by Margaret P. Pumphrey*      ISBN: *1-59462-116-0*   **$17.95**
*This book explores pilgrims religious oppression in England as well as their escape to Holland and eventual crossing to America on the Mayflower, and their early days in New England...*      History Pages 268

www.bookjungle.com *email: sales@bookjungle.com fax: 630-214-0564 mail: Book Jungle  PO Box 2226  Champaign, IL 61825*

**QTY**

**The Fasting Cure** *by Sinclair Upton*                                                ISBN: *1-59462-222-1*   **$13.95**
*In the Cosmopolitan Magazine for May, 1910, and in the Contemporary Review (London) for April, 1910, I published an article dealing with my experiences in fasting. I have written a great many magazine articles, but never one which attracted so much attention...  New Age/Self Help/Health Pages 164*

**Hebrew Astrology** *by Sepharial*                                                    ISBN: *1-59462-308-2*   **$13.45**
*In these days of advanced thinking it is a matter of common observation that we have left many of the old landmarks behind and that we are now pressing forward to greater heights and to a wider horizon than that which represented the mind-content of our progenitors...  Astrology Pages 144*

**Thought Vibration or The Law of Attraction in the Thought World**   ISBN: *1-59462-127-6*   **$12.95**
*by William Walker Atkinson*                                                                       *Psychology/Religion Pages 144*

**Optimism** *by Helen Keller*                                                          ISBN: *1-59462-108-X*   **$15.95**
*Helen Keller was blind, deaf, and mute since 19 months old, yet famously learned how to overcome these handicaps, communicate with the world, and spread her lectures promoting optimism. An inspiring read for everyone...  Biographies/Inspirational Pages 84*

**Sara Crewe** *by Frances Burnett*                                                  ISBN: *1-59462-360-0*   **$9.45**
*In the first place, Miss Minchin lived in London. Her home was a large, dull, tall one, in a large, dull square, where all the houses were alike, and all the sparrows were alike, and where all the door-knockers made the same heavy sound...  Childrens/Classic Pages 88*

**The Autobiography of Benjamin Franklin** *by Benjamin Franklin*   ISBN: *1-59462-135-7*   **$24.95**
*The Autobiography of Benjamin Franklin has probably been more extensively read than any other American historical work, and no other book of its kind has had such ups and downs of fortune. Franklin lived for many years in England, where he was agent...  Biographies/History Pages 332*

| Name | |
|---|---|
| Email | |
| Telephone | |
| Address | |
| | |
| City, State ZIP | |

☐ **Credit Card**          ☐ **Check / Money Order**

| Credit Card Number | |
|---|---|
| Expiration Date | |
| Signature | |

*Please Mail to:   Book Jungle*
*PO Box 2226*
*Champaign, IL 61825*
*or Fax to:          630-214-0564*

## ORDERING INFORMATION

**web**: *www.bookjungle.com*
**email**: *sales@bookjungle.com*
**fax**: *630-214-0564*
**mail**: *Book Jungle  PO Box 2226  Champaign, IL 61825*
**or PayPal** *to sales@bookjungle.com*

*Please contact us for bulk discounts*

## DIRECT-ORDER TERMS

**20% Discount if You Order Two or More Books**
Free Domestic Shipping!
Accepted: Master Card, Visa, Discover, American Express